BLOOD BROTHERS

Ernst Haffner

Blood Brothers

TRANSLATED
FROM THE GERMAN
BY

Michael Hofmann

Harvill *Secker*
LONDON

Published by Harvill Secker 2015

2 4 6 8 10 9 7 5 3 1

First published with the title *Jugend auf der Landstrasse Berlin* in 1932 by
B. Cassirer, Berlin. Reissued with the title *Blutsbrüder* in 2013 by Metrolit, Berlin

First published in Great Britain in 2015 by
HARVILL SECKER
20 Vauxhall Bridge Road
London SW1v 2SA

A Penguin Random House Company

Penguin
Random House
UK

global.penguinrandomhouse.com

A CIP catalogue record for this book is available from the British Library

ISBN 9781846558634 (hardback)
ISBN 9781846558641 (trade paperback)
ISBN 9781473511002 (ebook)

The Random House Group Limited supports the Forest Stewardship Council®
(FSC®), the leading international forest-certification organisation. Our books
carrying the FSC label are printed on FSC®-certified paper. FSC is the only
forest-certification scheme supported by the leading environmental
organisations, including Greenpeace. Our paper procurement policy
can be found at www.randomhouse.co.uk/environment

Typeset in Bauer Bodoni by Palimpsest Book Production Limited,
Falkirk, Stirlingshire
Printed and bound in Great Britain by
Clays Ltd, St Ives plc

BLOOD BROTHERS

ONE

Eight Blood Brothers – tiny individual links of an exhausted human chain stretching across the factory yard and winding up two flights of stairs – stand and wait among hundreds of others to be admitted from the awful damp cold into the warm waiting rooms. Just three or four minutes to go now. Then, on the dot of eight, the heavy iron door on the second floor will be unlocked. The local welfare bureaucracy for Berlin-Mitte on Chausseestrasse jerks into life; the coiled line jerks into life. Limbs advance, feet shuffle, hands clutch the innumerable necessary papers. (In the furtherance of good order, the office

1

has put out printed instructions that list them in endless sequence, and which twenty-four offices are responsible for issuing them.)

The queue has already reached the cash-office waiting room. There, with military precision, it splits into two smaller queues. One waits patiently to surrender its stamped cards to the hoarse-voiced office boy Paule, prior to receipt of payment. The second queue winds in front of the information counter in order to answer questions of who and where and where from, and then, with luck, to be issued with cardboard numbers. Thereafter, the individual parts will go into two other rooms to stand outside the doors of officialdom and wait with the patience of saints for their number to be called. The saints will have to be patient for five or six hours or more. The eight gang members join neither of the two queues but make straight for United Artists. Maybe they'll be in time for a bench.

The 'United Artists' waiting room, where applications for urgent assistance are filled in. The initials 'UA' have been repurposed by cynical Berlin humour as 'United Artists'. Half an hour after opening time, the large hall is already jam-packed. The few benches are fully occupied. Individuals who couldn't find a seat fill the aisles or lean against the two long walls, which have acquired a nasty black stain at shoulder height from so many thousands of slumped human backs.

The indescribably dreary light of the day outside mingles with the glow of the weak electric bulbs to form a chiaroscuro, in which these poor souls look even more wretched, even more starved. On the other side of the walls are bright clean offices. Though these offices are fitted with doors, in the conventional manner, beside each door there is also a four-sided hole large enough for the head of an official on a lower pay scale. To spare their vocal cords and to avoid excessive contact with the needy public, the officials don't themselves call out the numbers through the doors. No, a flap is thrust open, a human head appears nicely framed and yells out the number. And with that the flap clacks shut. The number – in the office, it is translated back into 'Meyer, Gustav' or 'Abrameit, Frieda' – trots into the office through the door beside the hole. Each time a number is called, all the waiting heads jerk up. It can happen that two numbers are called from opposite walls simultaneously. Then all the heads jerk up and back in time.

The eight boys were able to capture a whole bench and, serenely oblivious to the numbers, they drop off to sleep. They've spent the whole endless winter's night on the street. As so many times before: homeless. Always trudging on, always on the go. No chance of any shut-eye in this weather. Day-old remnants of snow, the occasional thin shower of sleet, everything nicely shaken up by a wind that makes the boys' teeth chatter with cold. Eight boys, aged sixteen to nineteen. A few are veterans of borstals. Two have parents somewhere in Germany. The odd one perhaps still has a father or mother someplace. Their birth and early infancy coincided with the war and the years after. From the moment they undertook their first uncertain steps, they were on their own. Father was at the Front or already listed missing. Mother was turning grenades, or coughing her lungs out a few grams at a time in explosives factories. The kids with their turnip bellies – not even potato bellies – were always out for something to eat in courtyards and streets. As they grew older, gangs of them went out stealing. Stealing to fill their bellies. Malignant little beasts.

Ludwig from Dortmund has jerked awake at the sound of a number being called. Now he's sitting there, feet out, fists in his pockets, empty cigarette holder in the corner of his mouth. The lantern-jawed face with the alert brown eyes looks with interest in the direction of the entrance. His friends are all asleep, slumped forward, collapsed, or leaning inertly against their neighbours. Jonny, their leader, their boss, has summoned them for nine o'clock. As so often before, he has promised to get hold of money from somewhere. He hasn't said how. At ten last night he said goodbye – at this point, Ludwig sees Jonny walking into the room, and he waves animatedly. 'Here, Jonny, over here!' Jonny is a young man of twenty-one. His physiognomy, with square chin and prominent cheekbones, looks a little brutal, and testifies to his willpower. He speaks with fluency and decisiveness, almost without dialect, and this proves that he stands above the rest of the gang in terms of education and intellect. Superior strength is taken for granted; he wouldn't be their boss otherwise. 'Hey, Ludwig!' He hands him a big box of cigarettes. Ludwig helps himself and chews on the smoke with delight. The others are still sleeping. Ludwig takes a long drag and blows smoke in their faces. They gulp, splutter, wake up. Nothing could have woken them so effectively. Cigarettes? Jonny? Here! Quickly all help themselves. And now they know too that Jonny's in the money, and that they're going to get something to eat. So what are they waiting for? As ever, they move in three troops. Nine boys in a gaggle attracts too much unfavourable attention. They turn off Chaussee- into Invalidenstrasse. That's where they buy breakfast. Forty-five rolls in three mighty bags, and two entire liver sausages with onion. That has to do for the nine of them.

Rosenthaler Platz, Mulackstrasse, then down Rückerstrasse. Into the bar used by all the gangs around the Alexanderplatz, the Rückerklause. You can stand outside and watch the cooks frying batches of potato pancakes. The greasy scraps of smoke drift into the furthest recesses of the unlit, sinister, and unsavoury bar. In spite of the early hour, it's already full. The Klause is more than just a bar. It's a kind of home from home for those who don't have a home. Noisy loudspeaker music, noisy customers. The unappetising buffet, the beer-sodden tables, the smoke-blackened graffitied walls – all this doesn't bother anyone. The gang occupy the space to the right of the door. The waiter brings them some broth – well, at least it's hot. Then they set about scoffing their rolls and liver sausage. There's not much conversation. Only dark, barbarous sounds: the grunts with which the stomach expresses its satisfaction. The boys are transformed. They sink their teeth into the sausage ends, they work their jaws. They look at each other, their expressions seeming to say: Don't it feel good to be eating, and knowing there's more to come . . . And other expressions, of gratitude and pride, are for Jonny, who once more has saved their bacon.

In one of the booths at the back, a young gang member is sitting on the lap of a passed-out customer. Two of his mates are walking up and down in front of the niche, gesturing to their chum: 'Go on, mate!' Pull the wallet out of his pocket, and give it to us . . .

Standing at the bar between two gang bosses is a

girl, a child of fifteen or sixteen. Cheekily she's put on the leather jacket of one of the young men, who doesn't need it, and his peaked cap, and is now tossing back one schnapps after another with the two of them. The sickly pale face with its blue veins at the temples convulses with disgust, but then the dirty little paw reaches for the glass to drink to one of the leather jackets. The girl's mouth opens: almost no teeth, just isolated blackened stumps. She's not even sixteen . . .

Behind the bar stands the watchful landlord. In a good blue suit and spic-and-span collar, the only one in the whole bar. Music blares out without a break. Incessant comings and goings. Everyone here is either young or underage. Many turn up with rucksacks and parcels. They go directly to the bathroom, the hideously dirty toilets. Brief exchange, unpacking, packing, money changes hands. A schnapps at the bar. Gone. Police raids are not infrequent.

The girl, legless by now, goes reeling from table to table, offering herself. Oh, Friedel, showing off again, they say, otherwise unmoved by the sorry spectacle of a drunken child offering her scrawny charms. Rückerklause, a kind of home from home for those who don't have a home. The forever-hungry boys have demolished the rolls and the liver sausage, and two potato pancakes each. They lean back contentedly, draw on their ciggies, sip their beer, and hum along to the tunes on the loudspeaker. '. . . *Auf die Dauer, lieber Schatz, ist mein Herz kein Ankerplatz . . .*' They're full, the bar feels warm. They're starting to feel drowsy. Their heads sink. Only Jonny is sitting up, smoking, watchful. He pays the tab for them all. Then he counts up what he's got left. All of eight marks. Where will they go tonight? The very cheapest hostel takes fifty pfennigs for the use of a bug-ridden mattress. That comes to four-fifty, which would mean almost nothing left for tomorrow. Jonny racks his brains for a cheaper option. Lets them sleep. He leaves word with the waiter to tell them to meet him at Schmidt's at eight.

TWO

The night-time equivalent to the Rückerklause is Schmidt's on Linienstrasse. Of course it's busy and there's a din of brass band music all day here as well. But, after dark, the bustling little bar becomes a throngging teeming scene. The beer tap isn't idle for a minute, and every chair is occupied twice over. And whoever hasn't got one at all leans against the stage or just stands anywhere he can, beer glass in hand. The inevitable paper chains, essential for producing a festive atmosphere, are permanently shrouded in thick tobacco fumes, even though a ventilator is doing its best to restore law and order to the air. The band plays energetically and without a break. Generous rounds of beer and shorts sustain them. Sustain them to the point that the alcohol starts to affect the tunefulness of their playing. That's when Schmidt's really comes into its own. Then the whole bar becomes one roaring foot-stamping chorus.

Jonny needs to dig up his eight fellows from various nooks and crannies to tell them he's scoped out a cheap billet for the night. Two marks for the whole lot of them. It's in a warehouse on Brunnenstrasse. For two marks the nightwatchman will let them in at ten. But at six o'clock tomorrow morning they'll have to be on their way again. Straw and large crates they can curl up inside are provided. At half past nine the gang set off.

On the stroke of ten, they're all close to the billet. Three of them are at the gate. The others are waiting nearby in the passage, to nip in the second the night-watchman opens the door. Before they even hear him, there's a furious growling and yapping behind the door: the guard dog. Then the door is unlocked, and one by one they sneak inside. The watchman locks the door after them. The bitch howls with rage and disappoint-ment. She doesn't understand her master. Normally she is under orders to go for anyone's legs, and just now, with this collection of deeply suspicious individuals, she is kept on a short leash. The nightwatchman slopes on ahead with the snarling dog. The Blood Brothers bring up the rear after a respectful interval. The door of the low storehouse is unbolted, and Jonny has to put down his two marks. Then the old man goes through all their pockets. He's looking for matches or lighters in case one of the scapegraces should get it into his head to smoke in there . . . With all that straw and dry wood around. That would be a right old firework. The guard dog tries a parting snap at the boys. But the studded collar reminds her that only non-paying guests are to be shredded. The boys are just finding their way round the dark windowless space when the old man locks them in. The freed dog sniffs crossly at the crack between the floor and the bottom of the door. Just let them try and get out . . .

The boys grope around in the dark. They catch themselves on nails, and as soon as someone thinks he's found a good spot, a few piled-up crates come crashing down about his ears. By the time everyone has found a place in a crate or on a bale of straw, it's striking eleven. In a few more minutes, they're all asleep. Only the mice are upset about the intrusion.

Were one able to see them, the huddled bodies of the boys in the crates and the straw, in their so-called beds, there would probably be only a voice of pity. Sixteen-year-old Walter, with his pigeon chest bulging out the front of his shirt and his Basedow pop-eyes

11

. . . And Erwin, also sixteen, a beanpole, whose stringy arms show not the merest trace of muscle. Or quiet, dreamy Heinz: he is using his jacket as a pillow, his shirt is a filthy rag. Ludwig, the eighteen-year-old from Dortmund who fled from the institution a year ago, has tunnelled so deeply into the straw that there's nothing of him to be seen, and the mice scamper across his body. The boys all look wretched. Only Jonny retains an expression of bold resoluteness, even in sleep.

In the pre-dawn dark of six, they're all standing out on Brunnenstrasse again. The cold they couldn't shake from their bones during the night now hurts like an acute pain. Frail Walter is gibbering so badly that they take him in their midst and make him jog-trot a ways to get him a little warmed up. Broken up into their usual sub-groups, they are heading for Alexanderplatz. To the Mexiko. That opens at six. A cup of hot broth, no matter how thin and stale, will do them the power of good.

Hands cupped round the mugs, the Blood Brothers sit in a corner, tanking warmth . . . PA music at a volume that would have gratified a symphony orchestra, from 6 a.m. till three o'clock the next morning. Pimps, prostitutes, gang members, wrestling associations, casual criminals and vagrants, bourgeois slumming it, and detectives looking for someone. That's the Mexiko. A few years ago, it was a small pub that failed for lack of custom. Now it proudly advertises as Europe's most prominent restaurant. The new owner clipped a few pictures of Indians from Moritz's picture book, and plastered the four walls of his premises with cheap and cheerful copies. Set out some artificial palm trees, painted over the windows so no one could see in or out, and called his work a Mexican cantina.

The Blood Brothers are sitting quietly at their table. Another day ahead of them. They face it without a plan. A man walks into the pub, a stranger, not a regular. Looks about him inquiringly, and makes for their table. The eighteen-year-old Fred, Jonny's lieutenant, leaps up, knocks a few of the others out of his way, and crashes out on to the street with the stranger in hot pursuit. Excitement in the establishment. What was that about? Police? But none of the customers has ever seen the man before. And they know all the local rozzers. The gang is puzzled. It feels inadvisable to stay any longer in this place. Jonny divides up the rest of the money equally, splits the gang up into four pairs, and sets them to look for Fred in all the usual places – with allied gangs, in hidey-holes. Even if he manages to get away from the stranger, Fred won't risk going back to the Mexiko. So he'll need to find out where the gang have got to. The rendezvous is eight o'clock at the homosexual bar the Alte Post on Lothringer Strasse. The four pairs head off in four different directions.

THREE

In the institution, the atmosphere has been mutinous for several days now. A small group, headed by the twenty-year-old Willi Kludas, have fixed on a kind of passive resistance. It was discussed at night in the dorm, and traitors and blacklegs were threatened with extreme measures: the sanctions were beating, beating and more beating. The director and educators were powerless in the face of the consequences of this passive resistance, up to and including acts of sabotage. Half the work gangs called in sick, suddenly people came down with the most obscure conditions. And the rest, while seeming to work, actually did more harm than good. The overseers were livid, threatened physical punishment or putting on report, but they were not able to prove any malicious intent. The youths smirked at each other as they put their heads down and went on 'working'. They were starting to enjoy themselves.

In the buildings, dozens of windowpanes inexplicably broke. Locks stuck. Workmen had to be hired to extract sand and grit from the works. In the bathrooms, toilets were blocked, electric lights and fuses burned out en masse. Documents and entire files disappeared, or blue ink was spilled over them. The boys couldn't wipe the grins off their faces. This was some campaign that Willi had come up with, this was something else. The educators went round with pale faces and gritted teeth. They no longer had the nerve to approach the director. Woe betide any boy they caught red-handed. But the system of lookouts worked, and everything the authorities tried was ineffectual or only made matters worse.

On the afternoon of the fourth day the director called the staff together. What's going on here? Yes, what is going on? They were baffled. Under the pretext of getting him to water some of the plants, they called in a boy – their boy, Georg Blaustein – to the director's room. 'Come on, Georg, you're a sensible boy, tell us what's going on. You've always kept us informed.'

Georg Blaustein was haunted by an apparition four nights ago. He was lying there awake, same as everyone else. Suddenly a face loomed over his from the darkness. 'If you breathe a word, I'll break your neck . . .' With that the face disappeared beneath Georg's bed, beneath several other beds, back to its own. 'I . . . I don't . . . I really don't know . . . sir, what . . .' Of course, the director and all the teachers could tell that Georg knew everything, and that fear was keeping his lips sealed. 'All right, Georg, do the plants.' Outcome: we don't know, but we know! Strict ban on smoking for all boys, no time off, exemplary punishments for all transgressions. Till the return of normality. Report to the supervising authority with a request for instructions.

And what was going on? What had caused the quiet uprising? An almost daily occurrence. Willi Kludas, the twenty-year-old charge, had been given a slap for some infraction by Herr Friedrich, the loathed trainer. It was Willi's birthday. He had taken it apparently without a murmur. But then in the night he had summoned up the quiet protest. As immediate retaliation. He wanted to get his own back on Herr Friedrich. For the repayment of the slap with interest, Willi had thought of a particular plan, in which he initiated only his six closest friends, whom he needed to put it into effect.

Two evenings later. Between ten and eleven o'clock. The whole dorm can sense that something is about to happen. But only seven boys, Willi and his six friends, know what it is. Half an hour earlier, the face had loomed up beside Georg Blaustein's bed again, and had uttered terrible warnings . . . Willi knows that if there's a commotion now, his friend Friedrich will come. And that's good. Very good. The seven boys, according to plan, embark on a noisy conversation, which gets louder and louder. Again according to plan, there's a knock on the door: 'Quiet in there!' Herr Friedrich's voice. Okay. Quiet. For a little while. Not too long. Suddenly the conspirators make a hellish row, the whole of the dorm sits up. Two of Willi's friends grab a sheet and trot off to the door barefoot. And here comes Herr Friedrich. The door flies open. A light switch clicks. No light. Two forms holding a sheet jump on Friedrich, who is standing in the doorway of the darkened room. Throw the sheet round his body. Four other boys hold the man by the hands and feet, a barely audible gurgling sound emerges from the sheet. Then Willi hurls himself at the white bundle. The whole room is silent, everyone hears the slapping sound of the blows. Then the boys whip the sheet off, and Herr Friedrich is deposited in the corridor. The door falls shut, and the avengers flit back to bed.

17

Half an hour passes – the sheets are all pressed nice and flat again – then in walk the director and several half-dressed but armed teachers. There is still no light. Two boys have to be roused from deep sleep. They are to fetch ladders and screw in new bulbs. Then at last there is light, and, surprise surprise, everyone is awake, staring at the pyjama-ed staff. The fact is that Herr Friedrich was beaten by several figures in nightshirts, not too badly. But which figures? The whole dorm says with one voice: 'I was asleep. The noise woke me.' Georg Blaustein outdoes everyone though. Not only was he not woken by the noise, no, he is so petrified he is still asleep. The investigation is suspended without result. Every one of the boys knows they are in for a collective punishment.

In the morning there are no work gangs. Everyone is confined to quarters for questioning. Notorious evildoers and teachers' pets are interviewed individually. The rest in small groups. The result of the inquiry is kept secret. Punishments have not yet been announced. It remains a grave case. The supervisory authority is being asked to send a commission of inquiry. Herr Friedrich has called in sick.

Tonight I'm making a break for it, Willi Kludas has decided. In a letter a boy will 'discover' tomorrow, Willi will claim sole responsibility. Those who helped him in the assault were press-ganged into it. He alone had beaten Herr Friedrich. The reason, sir? Because of the slap he gave me on my twentieth birthday. At lunch and dinner Willi eats everything he can lay his hands on. Who knows when he'll next get a meal. He will walk all night to the nearest main-line railway station. Then he will try and get to Berlin with a platform ticket. A ten-hour ride. How he proposes to remain undetected on the train he can't yet say. He takes discreet leave of his six friends. They give him some of their supper to take with him, and they hand over their spare change. Willi's cash holdings come to ninety-five pfennigs. An hour before bedtime he takes the decisive step. In an hour's time they will notice he's gone; by then he must be a long way away. Now his friends have to do him one last kindness. They stage an argument with no end of shouting and yelling. The now-skittish teachers and even the director himself rush into the day room. While the friends act confused, Willi hops over the wall.

He needs to run to the nearest settlement, which is ten minutes away. And then not through it, but round it. But not too quickly, so that he doesn't use up all his energy. Wow, does it feel good, running like that! Running and running, in a straight line. Not having to turn, like in the yard of the institution. With the grotty weather there's no one about, thank God. Willi runs with fists pumping and elbows tucked: 'One, two, three, four . . . one, two, three, four . . .' Ah, it feels grand. Wonder if they've noticed yet? Pray to God they don't send a teacher after him on a bike . . . One, two, three, four . . . hup, hup. Now left along the footpath, the village is on the right. Oh shit, the ground's boggy, great clumps of it are sticking to his soles. It makes a difference. Now don't slow. Hup, hup!

He's left the village far behind him, he's back on the main road. It's easier, running here. What about a break? No, another quarter-hour first. He's starting to get hot. Without stopping, he pulls a piece of bread out of his pocket . . . Smack, he's lying down in the roadside ditch. A car speeds past. Luckily, going the other way. On, on. Come on, Willi, come on! But finally he is running out of puff. A five-minute break. Behind the hedge. What I'd give for a cigarette . . . Am I not near the next village yet? Maybe I'll take a chance and buy five fags in the bar. Course I will! All right, Willi, let's go, the sooner you'll get your cigarette. One, two, three, four . . .

A girl's serving in the pub, and Willi gets his cigarettes. He treats himself to a slow walk for the first of them. But as soon as the butt is in the ditch, he breaks into a sprint. A cigarette is an amazing thing, isn't it, it gives you as much energy as a roast goose. Too bad he can't run and smoke at the same time.

But then he'd be sharing it with the wind. The skinny little thing would burn down in a flash. Hup, hup! They must be on to him by now, back home. Home? Some home! Prison is what it was. He turns off the road, and slows to a walk. Sufficiently far away from the road that he can keep an eye on it. Trotting along, the occasional smoke, thinking about what to do next. How do I get to Berlin? What if they nab me on the train? Then he'll be back in the institution the next day, and the courts will want to punish him for what he did to old Friedrich.

Five in the morning, completely knackered, he walks into the town. Maybe they're already waiting for you here, he thinks. As he approaches the station, he sees long lines of goods wagons in a siding. Well, the passenger express is no good to him, that's for sure, where's he going to lay low for ten hours? On the bog? The inspectors have got keys and all, and they're bound to look everywhere. He'll have to take the goods train. He scans the labels to see where it's going. Can't make head nor tail of it. So he up and jumps into a canvas-covered wagon. Bales of wood wool. He settles himself between two bales, arranges the makings of a pillow, and lies down. Who cares where they're going. Just get away from here, and sleep!

FOUR

Fred had every reason to go haring out of the Mexiko. The man he was running from was neither a stranger nor a policeman. Fred was running away from his old man. A postman from Schöneberg. Fred's mum has been dead for ages. The old man repeatedly threatened to abandon Fred and leave him to his fate, unless he stopped robbing family and friends. Fred had run away numberless times, numberless times his father had thrown him out after compensation for Fred's latest misdeed cost him another two weeks' wages. But no sooner was Fred gone for a couple of days than the old man would start looking for his son. For days on end. He had pulled him out of the Mexiko once before. Another time, the police had tipped him the wink. Then, once Fred was happily back at home, he would beat the living daylights out of him. But soon enough Fred would fall back into his old ways. He sold all his father's clothes, and one day his father had even caught him in the act of getting the piano picked up by a furniture dealer.

Today was another one of those days. He went looking for his son. Found him. Kept him in sight as Fred ran across Alexanderplatz. A succession of trams happened to cut off Fred's road. The old man caught him up. He didn't say anything on the street, but he kept a trembling grip on Fred's arm. Then they piled onto a bus, transferred to a number 5 at Stettiner Bahnhof, heading for Schöneberg. The old man fried him four eggs for breakfast and set the plate down in front of him. Pulled on his postie's jacket and locked Fred in the back bedroom. Neither of them said a dicky bird.

Fred sits in the fourth-floor bedroom. The doors to the room and the apartment are both locked. Run away, do one, back to the gang, of course that's all he can think about. But how's he going to get out? He doesn't even have a piece of wire to tickle the lock with. Damn. And the old man's chastisement tonight. Two, three hours go by. He can neither sleep nor sit

nor read. He's even let the eggs go cold. How's he
going to get out of here? He's just thrown himself
down on the bed when he hears the gang signal. A
whistle. He throws the window open. Walter and Erwin
are standing in the courtyard, craning upwards.
Looking questioningly, gesticulating. For a few seconds
Fred runs round the room in perplexity, then he scrib-
bles a note on a piece of paper: *The old man's locked
me in. Can you get hold of a bit of wire for me, for
a jemmy? So I can get the door open?* He secures the
note to an end of thread, and lowers it out of
the window. Walter and Erwin read it and scarper.
Fred stands by the window, waiting. The boys return
in triumph with three feet of wire, purchased at the
nearest ironmonger's. Fred pulls up the wire on
the end of his thread. Tries and tries to bend it with
his bare hands. He can't do it, it's too thick. He jams
one end of the wire between the drawer and a chest.
The wood suffers, but the wire bends in the desired
way. The primitive jemmy is ready. The simple
bedroom lock gives right away. There's the first. Now
it's the turn of the apartment door. A security lock,
no, that's not so easy, sunshine. Fifteen minutes go
by, half an hour. The lock won't budge. Fred is crying
with frustration. Then suddenly it does. A grind, a
squeak, a couple of clicks, and the apartment door is
open as well. Cap on, coat on. Fred stops for a minute,

runs into the open living room, and soon finds what he was looking for: his gold confirmation watch. He closes the front door behind him, and races down the stairs.

'Morning, gentlemen!' he greets his mates. Fred is full of glee, imagining the old man's face when he finds the apartment empty and notices that Fred hasn't left empty-handed either. He shows no hint of shame or doubt as he produces the stolen watch. It's his after all, innit? Sure, the old man bought it for him with his savings over many years, but a present is a present . . . The only question is whether he should hock it or flog it. The pawnbroker demands to see papers. That settles it then, he'll flog it, queer Christopher is certain to be interested.

Queer Christopher, a local fence in Schöneberg, is interested. He offers thirty marks, he knows any pawn-shop will offer him a hundred for the solid gold watch. He agrees to go up to forty. No more: he needs to keep his margins up. Fred pockets the forty marks; he would have taken twenty. First, he treats his mates to a slap-up dinner at Aschinger's. Then the three of them hop into a taxi to the Alte Post, on Lothringer Strasse.

All the Blood Brothers are there. Fred, the escaped hero, is welcomed with a great fanfare. The waiter has both hands full. Fred orders mulled wine, cigarettes and chocolates all round. And now Fred has to tell them all about it. Even his friends fall silent as he tells how the old man just 'gawped at me, like he was about to burst into tears . . .' In the long run, mulled wine is too expensive. Fred is in a mood to drink himself unconscious. But on the cheap. They go round Elsässer Strasse to one of the notorious Raband bars. Here you can get blotto at a competitive price. For ten pfennigs you can get a schnapps that'll scorch your throat like pepper. Fred calls for a round of doubles. He gives the command: 'Blood Brothers!' They take their glasses. 'Drink!' And they knock back the stuff. Next round. And another. 'Blood Brothers . . . drink!'

The drink has transformed the taciturn Heinz. He makes as much noise as the rest of them put together. 'Ten in a row? No bother!' he brags. Fred makes it happen. Ten glasses are set up in front of Heinz. 'Blood Brother . . . drink!' 'Drink . . . drink . . . drink,' orders Fred sadistically. After the fifth, Heinz falls off his chair like an empty glove. His young face is a crumpled white sheet, the contents of his last glass dribble out of his mouth. The others go on with their senseless drinking. Just before closing time two old bloated whores join them, and Fred treats them as well, to as much schnapps as their boozy necks can take. At closing time, the ladies talk business. Jonny,

Fred, the reawakened Heinz and Konrad are taken in tow by the old trouts, who are intent on taking them for the last of their money. Ludwig and the rest of them totter back to a hostel on Linienstrasse. They'll all meet up somewhere tomorrow.

The glory of the forty marks hasn't taken long to dim. One solitary round thaler has escaped the clutches of the ladies. In late afternoon, the gang assembles in the Münzhof. The thaler is converted into beer and cigarettes. Ludwig notices that Heinz is missing. 'Heinz had to go to the emergency ward,' Jonny says matter-of-factly. Back with the ladies, Heinz fell into his old boastful habits. He wanted to make up for his failure as a drinker by putting on a show with the women. What about five times? . . . The drunken ladies cacklingly availed themselves of the virile eighteen year old, and by the time their flabby thighs relinquished him, he was bleeding. A couple of hours later, Heinz was unable to walk. They had to take him in their midst and take him to emergency. Five hours later, he was apparently still there.

Fred, in such good earning form, has a new idea that must be good for at least three hundred marks. Only he needs three or four helpers. From his time as a male prostitute he has one faithful old admirer left. A very well-off butter merchant, who is surely good for a couple of hundred marks, especially if there

27

are four of them. Fred picks Jonny, Konrad, Hans and Erwin to help him. Then he goes to find a telephone. Comes back and tells them he's meeting Fritz in the Tiergarten at eight. The helpers' task is to catch them together in a compromising situation. The four seeming strangers are to act outraged and threaten to call the police. The terrified Fred will beg his merchant to secure their silence with a little bribe. And that is where the three hundred marks comes in. 'A doddle. He won't kick up, he's got a wife and kids.' So Fred concludes his presentation.

Very slowly, setting one foot down in front of the other, Heinz walks into the bar. His eyes are full of pain and the fear of mockery from his friends. Fred is about to oblige: 'Well, how's it hanging, you old eunuch!' But curtly and decisively Jonny puts a stop to it. Heinz tells them that the doctor wanted to keep him in hospital. Only when Heinz objected that he would be very well looked after at home did he finally let him go. Fred wants to leave now, and he decides to add Georg and Walter to the bunch, just to be on the safe side. Ludwig and Heinz agree to meet them at Schmidt's at eleven.

Heinz can hardly remain upright from pain and exhaustion, and gratefully accepts Ludwig's suggestion that they go back to the hostel. They pool their money. There's just enough for a bed for Heinz.

FIVE

Ludwig is standing in front of an Aschinger's at Stettiner Bahnhof, gazing at the imposing sausages in the window. 'I'm sure they wouldn't miss one . . .' he thinks to himself. A fellow draws up next to him. Probably a couple of years older, a little bit better dressed as well. He looks at Ludwig, looks in the window, looks at Ludwig again. Then: 'I expect you're hungry, eh? . . . Fancy earning half a mark?' 'Half a mark?' says Ludwig. 'How'd I do that?' The fellow shows him a ticket for the left-luggage office. Perhaps Ludwig could pick the piece up for him. Sure, it was his ticket, but he couldn't get away, he had to stay by the bus stop, he was meeting his friend off the bus any minute. Okay. Ludwig takes the ticket and a mark piece to pay the charge; the change is his. That comes to one pea soup with bacon, plus at least half a dozen rolls, Ludwig thinks to himself on the short walk to the station. Or maybe a couple of frankfurters for twenty-five pfennigs, and the rest on cigarettes. Even better, he says to himself, and he hands the ticket to the official: 'My case, please.' The official comes back without the case, and says, 'Just a mo,' and goes away again.

One or two minutes go by, then the official comes back, and he points at Ludwig and says, 'It's him'. Someone taps Ludwig on the shoulder from behind: 'Would you mind coming along with us?' A transport policeman. The left-luggage official hands over to a colleague, and comes along to the police station as well. The duty officer listens to him first. He says: 'The ticket this young man presented was reported as lost earlier this morning. A gentleman claims he had it in his wallet, which was stolen from him on the tram.'

Ludwig is incensed: 'It's not me . . . there was this stranger I met outside Aschinger's . . .' 'All right, all right. One thing at a time,' the duty officer cuts him off. 'Have you got any identification, passport or regis- tration certificate?' he asks. 'No, not on me,' says Ludwig. 'All right, what's your name, then?' Ludwig hesitates. Should he give the officer his real name?

Then they'd send him straight back to the institution. Whereas if he gives a name that's not on any of the files, they'll just let him go. 'Erich Müller,' he says hurriedly. The officer writes it down. Ludwig gives him a made-up date of birth, and improvises other details. 'Address?' asks the officer. 'Homeless, just arrived in Berlin yesterday, looking for work.' 'So where're your papers then?' 'Er . . . I lost them yesterday on the way to the city.' The official seems to take it equably enough. 'All right, now give me your version of what happened again.' At last, Ludwig is able to launch into his account. He does it with such zeal that the official can't help but accede to Ludwig's earnest request to have an officer accompany him back to Aschinger's to identify the responsible party. Not least as it's one of the oldest tricks in the book, to get some third party to present the hot ticket.

Ludwig and a detective in civilian clothes make a large detour round the possibly still waiting villain to the spot where Ludwig was first accosted. He keeps his eyes peeled, but there's no one who looks even vaguely like the youth. The policeman is smirking. Wouldn't you know it, it was that A.N. Other again. Why couldn't the lads at least come up with something original once in a while? Back at the station, the statement is concluded. 'Are you adamant that you were to present the ticket on behalf of a third party, then?' 'Yes.' 'Very well, you're staying the night here in the station, and tomorrow morning you're being transferred to HQ,' says the policeman, and Ludwig is taken to a holding cell.

Thoughts are swarming and tangling in Ludwig's brain. Should he tell them that his name's not really Müller, and that he's fled from welfare? Then they won't believe another word he says. They'll think he's definitely the thief. But the police will surely work out by themselves that he's given them a false name.

An endless night on a hard wooden bench in the company of snoring drunks, night birds and arrested criminals. A continual lurching between half-sleep and panic each time someone else is thrown into the cell. Finally, in the early morning, the detainees are taken away by a police escort. Off into the van that does the rounds of the police districts, the Green Minna. The thing's already full to bursting when Ludwig is escorted out. He's put between two drunken women who're not too proud to grope him for cigarettes. The van rumbles off to HQ. In the yard, it does an elegant turn, and stops directly in front of a flight of steps going down to a basement. Under the watchful eye of the police, the freight, now separated into male and female, is taken to a large pen.

Hours and hours go by. The exhausted detainees are already reconciled to their misery and are exchanging

32

stories of the various prisons of their acquaintance. Presumptive sentences are passed. 'What did yer do?' 'Took the wallet off a john,' says a male prostitute. 'Any previous?' 'Nah.' 'Well, two, three months, on probation.' Thus the semi-professional judge. A sergeant comes along and calls out two or three names to the examining magistrate. Including Erich Müller.

A bare chilly office. Seated at his desk, cursorily looking up through his glasses, the magistrate. To one side a typist, young and pleasant, a faint scent of powder and good soap wafts over to Ludwig. 'So you're the young man with no papers, name of Erich Müller?' begins the magistrate. 'Born on —, last living at —. Is that right?' 'Yes, sir,' replies Ludwig, looking at the tapered white fingers of the typist, nimbly and efficiently feeding a fresh sheet of paper into her typewriter. 'Now what was the story with the ticket? Tell me in your own words.' 'Erich Müller' talks; the magistrate stands, feet apart, behind the desk, apparently listening intently.

Ludwig finishes his truthful account. The room is quiet inside, though the din of Alexanderplatz can be heard outside. The typist has spotted a blemish on the nail of her right index finger, and is just deciding to invest her money in a careful and painstaking manicure. The magistrate is still quiet, flexing a metal ruler into a semicircle. Then, very suddenly and roughly, he barks out a question to Ludwig: 'So you continue to claim your name is Erich Meyer, right?' Ludwig replies with a quiet, 'Yes, sir'. A short pause. 'Got you.' The magistrate sits down in triumph. Ludwig and the typist look up at him questioningly. 'In your statement you said your name was Erich Müller. A moment ago I asked whether you insisted your name was Erich Meyer. You said yes. How many names have you got?' The magistrate leans back in his chair. The blood rushes to Ludwig's head so fast that his eyes go black. The typist smiles foolishly. Now she too has registered her boss's trick. 'I would like to draw your attention to the fact that claiming a false identity carries severe penalties. Now, I want the truth.' Ludwig hooks his fingers in between the slats of his chair, the magistrate's voice is coming from a vast distance. 'Could I . . . have a glass of water?' The typist brings him one. The magistrate waits patiently. He knows his seed will bear fruit. 'My name is Ludwig N— and I'm a runaway from the home in H—.' The magistrate picks up the wanted list and scans it. 'Could be. When did you abscond from H.?' Ludwig gives the date, which matches the date on the sheet. The magistrate is now convinced that Ludwig is telling the truth. Since Ludwig is sticking to his story about the ticket, the hearing is at an end. The files of Ludwig N. are ordered from H. What happens next is up to the prosecution authorities. A red form is filled in. A form of destiny. An arrest warrant. A bell rings: take him away.

A sergeant walks Ludwig to the prison office. He is to wait in an area separated from the office by a chest-high partition. 'Have you got any money or valuables on you?' asks the official. Ludwig hands him the mark he was given by the hoodlum. Then he is taken away to prison. In front of him the endless corridor, left and right indistinguishable, cell by cell. Brown iron-clad door by brown iron-clad door. Only the numbers of the doors, which are the same as the numbers of the inmates, change. In the reception area, Ludwig is called upon to empty his pockets. Everything is taken off him. Then he is brought to a cell, and he's on his own. A rock-hard rumpled field bed, with blue-and-white sheets and two woollen blankets. A stool, a wall-mounted shelf for his tin dish, a drinking cup and a water jug. In the corner a stinking toilet. There's no space for a table.

The hobnails of the guards clank along the stone-flagged corridors. An eye looks through a peephole in the door, watches the inmates on the toilet or dreaming of freedom and girls . . . A jangle of metal against Ludwig's cell door. The insertion of a big key into the lock hits him like an electric shock. 'Come on.' He is handed over to a civilian official, who is to take him to get processed.

Upstairs and down, round corners and into obscure nooks of the huge labyrinthine building. A large bright room on the ground floor. Trams whizz past outside. 'Go in there.' Ludwig is shown into a cage of loose wire, next to a whimpering little girl. Almost a child. Wonder what she's done? Whatever it was, she is measured, fingerprinted, photographed from the front and both sides, as though she is a dangerous criminal. Ludwig's turn next. He has to wash his hands. 'Otherwise your sweat might blur the prints,' the official explains. He takes Ludwig's right hand, and gently presses the fingertips on a plate, which has previously been impregnated with printer's ink. Then he takes Ludwig's fingers one at a time, and presses each one in a space on the prepared personnel-data sheet. And then the same thing with the left hand. The prints of all ten fingers on both hands are to be kept for perpetuity. Then the photograph. A white draped room. Ludwig has to sit on a square stage. Rods at his back make him sit up straight, at both sides the delinquent model is kept in an upright posture. A flash of light. One profile is in the bag. The official pulls a lever. Ludwig, not having moved, is now full-face. The procedure a second time, with cap, then Ludwig is taken back to his cell.

SIX

Willi Kludas is woken by a terrible pressure. A heavy object is lying on top of him, crushing the breath out of him. Broad awake, he opens his eyes. He can see nothing, nothing at all. Below him something is going rat-ta-ta-TA . . . rat-ta-ta-TA. It takes Willi a while to get his bearings. Yes, he ran away, climbed into a railway wagon, and lay down among the wood wool. And it's a dislodged bale of wood wool that's crushing him. It's too big for him to lift. He twists and wrestles with difficulty until he's lying on his stomach, and slowly wriggles clear of the bale. When he lifts the heavy tarpaulin at the back of the wagon, he finally sees that it's night-time. The train is idling along.

In the brake hut of the wagon behind his own, Willi suddenly sees a little spark moving around and flaring. A smoking railwayman? Or a stowaway, like himself? Hurriedly, he re-secures the tarpaulin and squeezes down among the bales again. It's warmer there as well. He's still got a cigarette and a couple of squashed slices of bread. But nothing to drink. He smokes the cigarette first, careful not to get too near the wood wool. Where is the train going? The passing landscape gives no clues. And how long has he been travelling for? The locomotive whistles, then twice more, and the brakes start to squeal. No approach. Willi twists his way up, in the hope of maybe spotting the name of a station. The train has stopped in the middle of nowhere.

Cautiously Willi peeks through a finger-wide crack in the direction of the brake hut. The door opens, and a hatless head can be seen peering in all directions. There is no sign of any railway personnel. Now the man clambers down from the hut, stops at the bottom to look about him, and then slaps his arms round his ribs to warm up. Willi's eyes drill into the darkness to try and make out the figure. Slowly, slowly, he can make out a bearded face, a jacket, and a pair of track-suit bottoms with puttees. No sign of a railwayman's uniform. Should he call out to the fellow? Perhaps he can tell him where they are. On an impulse, Willi pushes up the tarpaulin and softly calls out: 'Psst, mate, over here!' The form jumps, makes to run off. Willi calls out a second time, and leans out. The tension leaves the man's body, and he comes closer. Willi pulls up the tarpaulin invitingly, and with a single bound the stranger is up with him. When the tarpaulin has been reattached, the bearded man pulls out a torch and shines it in Willi's face. What he sees seems to calm him down. 'Journeyman?' he asks. 'No,' replies Willi, 'I'm on my way to Berlin.' The man laughs. 'Berlin, eh? By the time it gets light, we'll be in Cologne!'

The news comes as a shock to Willi. Cologne? What would he do in Cologne? He doesn't know a soul there. That means he's been going in the wrong direction all this time. Would it be best to jump off now, while the train is stopped? No, there's no point. 'Does it have to be Berlin?' asks the stranger. 'Yes, I know someone there who'll help me out,' replies Willi. 'There is a way of getting to Berlin quickly and for no money,' says the stranger, 'but it's dangerous. I know some who've fallen on the tracks and been turned into cat food.' Willi asks what it is. Says he's ready for everything. Here in the Rhineland, the only alternatives are starving to death and turning himself in to the police. In Berlin he knows the ropes. Things will be better. But he needs to get there quickly. It could take a week or more on a goods train. The stranger shines his torch in Willi's face again. 'Don't go anywhere, I'll just get my pack out of the brakeman's hut.'

No sooner is he back than the locomotive whistles again. The train moves off. Willi and the stranger join forces to heave the bales out of the way, to give themselves more space. The stranger introduces himself to Willi. In spite of his beard, he's only thirty, is Franz, tramp from conviction, wanting to see Cologne again, where he hails from. Could be that Franz will be in Berlin in another week. Who can know? Willi volunteers that he's fled from borstal. Franz is busy doing something in the dark. The next time the torch flashes on briefly, Willi sees a bundle of newly rolled cigarettes in Franz's cap, rolled in the pitch black. Christ, the fellow's skilled. And then, when the two of them are smoking, Franz comes out with his plan of getting Willi to Berlin in quick time. There's a little pause for effect, then he says curtly: 'The express.' 'Get away!' says Willi in his disappointment. 'No, I'm serious, the express!' Franz insists. 'But what about the inspector, for Christ's sake!' objects Willi. 'You don't get no inspectors there. They're all up in the train.' Franz laughs. 'You're underneath the train.' Willi freezes. Under the express, at sixty mph? Never! Where is 'there', anyway? Under the carriages? Where do you hang on to when it's racing along?

Franz takes his time. Long before departure, when

40

the train is still in a siding, the stowaway has to climb under the train and hunker over an axle. That's where he has to hang, a foot or two above the ground. If he drops off, he's dead. But there's a chance, too, that a fist-sized chunk of ballast could bounce up and kill him. Or that his arms and legs seize up with cold or lack of movement, and can't hold him up on the axle any more . . . The prospects as Franz describes them aren't exactly rosy. He admits that he only takes this route when he's really up against it. His most horrible experience under an express was going from Warsaw to Berlin one time. From Warsaw to Berlin under the express! 'For cowards I expect it's easier to take a goods train,' Franz concludes. 'I'll take the chance,' Willi determines. It doesn't sound especially heroic, but it's a decision, and Willi is determined to follow it through. Franz offers to put Willi under the right train in Cologne – a city Willi doesn't know – and also offers to help equip him for the ride. Franz doesn't pursue the conversation, and Willi's thoughts are too preoccupied with the risk he's staring at. The train goes on with its monotonous rat-ta-ta-TA . . . rat-ta-ta-TA . . . rat-ta-ta-TA . . .

When they wake up from their nap, light is seeping through cracks in the tarpaulin. Franz pushes his way through to find out where they are. 'It's almost time, laddie. As soon as the train starts to slow, we'll hop off. How are you feeling about Cologne–Berlin now?'

Franz alludes to their earlier conversation. 'My mind's made up,' replies Willi. The locomotive whistles and starts to brake. There's still no trace of Cologne, they're just going through a little wood. Franz gives Willi instructions on how to jump off a train. Throw yourself down as soon as you land, so that the brakemen don't notice. The train slows further. Franz jumps first, and throws himself to the ground. Willi comes after. But he doesn't even need to throw himself to the ground, the impetus does it for him, he doesn't have much say in the matter. They set off across the fields, and before long they hit a tree-lined road. After a good hour or so, they reach the end of one of the tramlines, and not long after they're in the city.

Willi isn't especially interested in Cologne or the Rhine. He wants to get to Berlin. Franz, however, is full of the joys of coming home. Though Franz knows Willi is probably down to his last fifty pfennigs, he takes him along to his old hostel. Comradeship is a given among kings of the road. In the hostel they are shown to a niche with two field beds in it, and in the dining room there is a huge bowl of bean soup with pork belly. Willi starts to object again. 'Eat,' replies Franz, and divvies the meat up. When they are both full, Franz returns to the subject of Willi's trip. 'First you need to be well-rested. Otherwise you won't last an hour before you're ground up.' On Franz's advice,

Willi decides not to go till tomorrow night. Then they repair to their beds, to catch up on their sleep.

Willi sleeps through till noon the next day. He's planning to leave in the evening. After eating, they go back upstairs to prepare for the journey. In just five hours, he'll be lying on the axle. Franz has got hold of an old threadbare blanket, which he cuts up into pieces. Willi stands there, shaking his head. What's Franz doing, cutting up these yards and yards of foot-cloths? And that bag he's sewing? Franz drapes the bag over Willi's head, and marks the places for his eyes. Takes it off him again, and cuts a couple of peepholes in it. Two strips are sewn on to the bottom end. Finally Franz explains: 'You have to keep this bag over your head right through the journey. First, it'll keep you warm. Second, if you didn't have it, you'd arrive in Berlin with grime on your face an inch thick, and that would give you away.' Willi can imagine what a pair of heavy mittens would be for. But all those strips of material? Franz goes on to explain that in addition to his face his clothes will be filthy. So he needs to wear his anorak inside out, same with his trousers. In Berlin he'll just turn them right way round so he doesn't catch people's attention from the outset.

The strips of material are to be wrapped round legs, thighs and torso. On account of the cold, laddie! The cold times a sixty-mph wind. With your thin undergarments you'd be stiff as a board in no time, no feeling in your limbs, and the train wheels would grind you up. Obediently Willi takes off his outer garments, and allows himself to be wound about with the strips of blanket. Not too tight, mind, so that the blood can flow, but not so loose that they slip. Puts his trousers back on inside out, weskit and jacket over them, and then his anorak, again inside out. It barely fits over his jacket. Just before they head off for the shunting yard, Willi has to down a few glasses of schnapps. Their purpose is to keep his courage up and his blood going round.

It takes minute knowledge of the terrain to approach the already-prepared Cologne–Berlin train without being seen. As long as they're not on the actual rails, the wintry dusk keeps them from sight. But thereafter, they have to creep, crawl, slither and leap, taking advantage of every inch of shadow. Done it, thank God! They scurry along the side of the carriages. Not too near the back, there's too much lateral movement. But not too close to the front either, otherwise the locomotive might spew glowing ashes over the hapless bundle cowering under the carriage. Franz stops at a second-class carriage. Nothing but the best, Willi thinks to himself. They creep right up to it, and Franz demonstrates the way he has to hunker over the broad axle. Then he pulls out two short ropes from his pocket, and attaches them to a couple of bars. Now Willi has a couple of handholds. Once again, Franz does the demonstration, and Willi shows him he can do it. With the train standing still, it looks straightforward. Once he's in Berlin, Franz continues, best to hop off in some suburb, when the train's waiting for the track to clear. On no account go into a station, that's far too risky. Otherwise, wait till the passengers have all got off and the train is being put by. 'All right then, sunshine, best of luck!' Willi gets into his crouch, and gives his friend a firm handshake. Franz slopes off.

For a long time nothing happens to suggest the train is due for imminent departure. But then a huge express locomotive passes by, and is coupled to the front of the train. Willi feels the jolt run through the line of carriages. Soon after, some people walk by, the train crew. And then, with restrained power, the train moves off. The station is close. From the echoing sound of voices and rapid footfall, Willi Kludas can tell that they're in the station hall. He can't see anything, except if he lowers his head to the level of the axle and looks diagonally up. Feet going by, feet and legs about to climb into his carriage.

Willi becomes aware of a series of chimes. He sidles across to the far side of his axle. It's the guard walking alongside the train, striking the wheels with a hammer, checking for any flaws that might give rise to a disaster at high speed. Suddenly Willi can feel himself praying for something. If they get you now, you'll be in a prison cell within an hour. Maybe not that alluring, but if they don't spot you, you could be a nasty mess on the tracks instead. An icy shudder goes through him. He has to press his trembling hands hard to the cold iron to master his fear. A couple of feet away, there are people in idle conversation, sending regards to Uncle and Auntie. A warm soft woman's voice implores her 'sweetheart' for goodness' sake not to sit in the draught and catch his death of cold. Willi sees a pair of ladies' shoes, and shapely calves. Boy oh boy, if she knew someone was looking up her skirts . . . He has to laugh, and that gets rid of the fear. He feels a little impatient. Come on now, let's get the show on the road! It's getting boring here.

'All aboard! . . . All aboard, ladies and gentlemen!' The train crew rush from carriage to carriage, banging on the doors. The stockinged legs get up on tiptoe for a farewell kiss. Willi adjusts his position. Tomorrow morning you'll be in Berlin. That's all there is to it. Gently the train moves off. Slowly it glides out of the station hall. Now there are points, lots of sets of points. Each one is a little jolt. The train is still going slowly, but Willi understands that, as soon as the suburbs are left behind, it will start racing. With considerable diffi-culty, he has managed to light a cigarette. It took half a box of matches before he could get the cigarette alight in the lee of his open anorak. All right, now. Let's go! And they're off. The glittering spokes of the wheels are flying round . . . then there's no more spokes, just whirling disks. Ouch! A pebble flies up and strikes him. Time for Willi to pull the blanket bag over his head.

The train has a clear track ahead and is flying along. Willi feels mild shocks, more in the nature of a rocking motion. Hands in the swinging handholds, legs pressed fast to the rods. By and by, Willi starts to feel the penetrating cold, the knife of the whistling wind. Thick dust comes in through his eyeholes. Turn the bag round, so the holes are at the back. Now Willi can't see a thing. What would be the point? He knows how to cling on. It's all he can do. Sit there and wait it out, just wait it out. Keep telling himself, tomorrow morning you'll be in Berlin. Keep telling himself something. Count from one to ten thousand. Or recite a poem, for Chrissakes. Only don't drop off, otherwise he'll have had his chips. A slight movement to one side or the other and he's a goner!

The icy wind drills deeper and deeper into his clothes, bites under the strips of material wound round his trunk. The body hanging there, stock still, loses its flexibility, becomes numb. Willi can no longer feel his hands cramping in their handholds, he can no longer move his fingers. He can't even feel himself hanging on the axle. All he feels is his body hurtling along at incredible speed, as though shot from a gun. He feels the occasional dull thump of a stone hitting him, but it's not a pain as such. He is released from his physical self, from time and space. How long has he been hanging like this? Is it one hour, is it four?

From the pitch of the wind he can tell that the train is slowing down. He adjusts his head protection a little: light and shade hurtle past, then the train clatters over points. They are entering a big station. Willi takes advantage of the few minutes they are stopped to move his limbs as much as possible in the constricted space. He alters his position. By leaning against a box under the carriage, he gets into a sort of seated position that allows him to shift his limbs around slightly while they are moving. He peers through the narrow chink between the carriage and the platform. Nowhere is the name of the place, and he doesn't hear it called out either. Nowhere in his limited field of vision a clock. Only legs, legs that won't tell him one thing or the other. 'All aboard . . .!' The train slips out, and quickly and ravenously chews into a racing speed.

But lest you think things can't get any worse, Willi Kludas . . . Lest you think it's a straightforward matter, cheating the railway of the price of a Cologne–Berlin ticket . . . you've got another think coming! What prompted you to lay into your well-intentioned educators, and then duck out of the punishment that was coming to you? Punishment? Hear that? Punishment? Yes, indeed. It'll catch up with you here, under the chasing express. Here. A rigid lump clinging on for dear life to still-colder iron! At last the resistance of your thick skull is broken. Cry, howl in the din. No one will ever hear you, not even the people sitting a few feet away on upholstered benches. Your desire for freedom, your longing to grope a girl in a passageway, to walk through the lit-up streets at night as a free man, not to be a youth any more, cuffed with impunity by anyone with half a mind to. All those desires that a careful education tried to repress in you, to make you a person after its own liking, you now must pay for with the price of this night in which death will not shrink from your side, not for a second!

The train rumbles over more points, and stops reluctantly at a signal. A child leans out of a carriage window and a joyful treble calls out into the morning: 'Mama . . . we're almost in Berlin!' The child's voice breaking the silence, the word 'Berlin' . . . together they mobilise the last resources in Willi Kludas so that he can crawl away from under the carriage. He collapses among some piles of wooden sleepers. The train moves off with a jerk and is soon gone. Willi bestirs himself. He can't stay here. Over there are long lines of empty carriages on dead tracks. That's where he has to get himself to.

He can't walk upright. Crawling and slithering like a stoned dog, Willi moves in the direction of the carriages. On the way is a barrel of rainwater. Water, water for his parched throat! It takes infinite effort to pull himself up at a carriage, to heave aside the door, to haul himself into the wagon, and finally to slide the door shut. Almost instantly, Willi slumps into wet straw that has been put there for a horse transport.

Late in the afternoon, as floodlights again brighten the sidings, Willi Kludas awakens to the torments of hunger and thirst. The awareness of having got through the ghastly night helps him overcome the pain in his bones. In the darkness of the wagon he gets undressed. He strips off the bandages that have served him well, knocks some of the dirt off his trousers and anorak, and pulls his things on right way round. He wipes his boots with handfuls of straw. Then he cautiously pushes the door open and peers out. No one there. In the dim light of distant lamps he studies his reflection. Good God! In spite of the head protection, his whole face is coated with a thick layer of grime. Carefully Willi crawls up to the water barrel again, and scrubs face and hands with water and grit. Another look in the mirror tells him that he isn't clean, but at least he's not so strikingly dirty that he will draw attention to himself when he's among people again.

Now, the thing is to get off the railway terrain

unobserved. Past the signal boxes, the railwaymen's quarters. Any shadow might harbour a railway official. Slithering and crawling, Willi crosses the rails, then he has to pass a signal box. He can clearly make out a couple of officials in the room, green and red lights flashing on and off. Past them. Now up a steep embankment, a careful straddle of a barbed wire fence, and he's all alone on an empty footpath. A passer-by tells him where to catch a tram into the city.

Berlin, Berlin . . . The name sounds like music to his ears. As if Berlin were a laid table and a soft bed waiting for Willi Kludas. He's got two cigarettes left, and twenty-five pfennigs. The first cigarette is lit. After the first deep puff, he almost moans with delight. Ah, cigarettes are something else. He contemplates jogging to the tram stop. But his aching bones refuse any fresh abuse. So he walks on.

It's about half past six when Willi gets off the tram in Müllerstrasse. He wants to look up a school chum. Maybe his mum will let Willi spend a night there. It's three years since Willi was last in Berlin. Pray to God that Otto Pageis is still living in Müllerstrasse. What was the number again? Here, this is the building, surely. And there's the greengrocer's cellar where they cadged bruised apples and pears when they were kids. Second yard, fourth floor, middle apartment, that's Otto's place, isn't it? But now he sees the name

'Kowalski' on a piece of card. All the same, Willi knocks. A slatternly, highly pregnant woman answers. 'Pageis . . . Pageis, yeah, there were people living here by that name. But they left. Thing is, she kept bringing so many gentlemen home, and the landlord wouldn't stand for it. And then they took Otto, the boy, and stuck him in welfare . . . yeah, that's what happened.' 'So, Otto's in welfare . . . thanks ever so much, ma'am . . .' Otto Pageis was the only person in Berlin that Willi knew to look up. And now he's in some institution himself, dreaming of Berlin . . .

Downstairs at the baker's Willi buys rolls with his last twenty pfennigs, and scarfs them down. Where'll he go for the night? Hard to answer. He can't run around much more, that's for certain. He sees nothing of the bustle of Müllerstrasse as he staggers on. He isn't drawn to the lights at the northern end of Friedrichstrasse either. Willi turns off, and wanders along the River Spree. It's half past nine already. Should he go to the Tiergarten? He can feel the cold settling in his bones. He can't go on much longer.

At Kronprinzen Ufer, he comes upon a sandbox marked 'BATG 2'. It's half full. Willi climbs into it, and shuts the heavy lid over his head. He smokes his last cigarette, then he burrows down into the wet sand. The great and compassionate city of Berlin has afforded a bed for Willi Kludas . . .

SEVEN

Ulli is the boss of a gang that's allied to the Blood Brothers, and it's his birthday. He's come of age, twenty-one today. Which means that remand schools and borstals have lost all their terrors so far as he's concerned. A great and long-awaited experience, worthy of a great celebration. Which is scheduled for tonight. Ulli has extended invitations to all the Blood Brothers. Starting at eleven o'clock, at intervals of fifteen minutes and in groups of three, the Blood Brothers are to wait at the corner of Koloniestrasse and 80th Street, Section 2. There they will be picked up by a boy and taken to the festive premises. No more than three at a time, so that the police don't get interested. The rest of the lads are to bide their time in a doorway on Koloniestrasse till it's their turn.

Jonny, Konrad and Erwin are the first. On the dot of eleven they're standing by a lamp post bearing the street sign *80th Street, Section 2*. Only thing is, there's no actual street by that name. After four paces in the direction indicated, a credulous so-and-so would find himself perched on top of a barbed-wire fence instead of turning down any street. Why, and to what purpose, that sign has been affixed to where it is, that's the sweet secret of the planning department of the city of Berlin . . . No one to be seen far and wide. There's no buildings yet, in these latitudes. Waste ground, gypsy caravans; summer houses, large and small; rotted planks and fences that decades of practice have kept in position. This is home to Ulli and his boys. A part of the world that might have been invented for discreet and silent disappearances.

Here comes Ulli's envoy. They've seen each other before. Somewhere between the planks and the barbed wire, there's a little gap. The four boys skip through it, and find themselves in deep mire. In Indian file, each holding on to the coat-tails of the one before, their guide leading the way, the group feel their way through the dark. Their feet plod through little ponds, get snarled up in discarded mattresses, stumble over

54

pots and pans and other detritus. Something runs across their path that was never a path; it could have been a cat or a rat or a rabbit. At last they get to a dark summer house. Their guide whispers the password through the keyhole: 'Hungry bellies, parched throats.' The doors are thrown open to hunger and thirst.

The sudden incursion of fresh air has brought turmoil to a thick fug of tobacco. The atmosphere is as dank as in a laundry. Ulli, the birthday boy, accepts congratulations and small contributions, and calls on them to be seated. Slowly the new arrivals adjust to the smoke. There is no furniture as such. There wouldn't be any room anyway. A few blankets and potato sacks have been spread over the bare floorboards, and the birthday guests sit and squat and sprawl over them. Against the wall is an upended orange box, with a three-foot altar candle set on it, burning. Next to that a good dozen or so full bottles of schnapps and wine. Against the opposite wall, muffled under a horse blanket, a gramophone. The guide sets off to pick up the next batch of Blood Brothers. In due course, they and the last pair settle themselves, rather intimately, on a potato sack. 'No Ludwig?' asks Ulli. Jonny tells him: 'He's disappeared for a week now. No one has any idea where he can have got to . . .' The conclusion that Ludwig's disappearance is involuntary is one they have all come to by now. The police have nabbed him, they think.

Sixteen gang members are assembled in the summer house. Someone puts a record on the gramophone, and covers it over again with the horse blanket. '*Hoch soll er leben*!' it drones out from under. Applause for Ulli. A bottle of cognac does the rounds. The last boy gets the grisly lees. 'Parched throats!' Parched throats of lads from fifteen to eighteen. Only a couple are older. Is it showing off, their thirst for alcohol? The cognac is chased with a bottle of plum brandy. It too is drained. Then cigarettes are passed round. From outside the door is unlocked. The sentry is relieved. Each one does half an hour. A dance tune animates them all to quiet whistling and humming along.

The altar candle shines, struggling with the smoky air. It's attached to a piece of string that runs along a wall, then feeds through the keyhole to somewhere outside. A simple and silent alarm system. If a stranger should approach the summer house, maybe the night-watchman or even the police, then the sentry will give it a yank: the candle will fall over. Darkness. Everyone is to keep quiet. But who would come now, in the middle of the night?

By way of a change, and to settle the hungry bellies, cooking chocolate is passed round in hefty slabs. Every man sinks his teeth in the marks left by his predecessor.

Ulli, now in his maturity, reminisces about his years of implacable struggle with the police, the welfare authorities, the educators in the borstals. They refused to allow him freedom, streets, bars, waste ground, girls. So he fought back. With hands and feet against his confining enemies. 'Die of hunger, sure! But at least where I wanna be!'

The sound of voices outside. The sentry's, yes, but a couple of others' as well. But the alarm candle stands there stubbornly. Ulli reaches across and dinches it. Choked cries from outside, the voice of the sentry: 'Ulli . . . Ulli, everyone out!' The door is locked, the sentry has the key. Rip the rags from the covered window! Ulli forces his way through, he's out. Four other lads after him. They'll do. Outside, a brief struggle, fought out in near silence. The sentry is freed and opens the door. The five who liberated him drag a couple of strangers into the summer house. A fresh sentry is posted, the candle is relit. Pull the boys into the light. Ah, they're no strangers. Members of a rival gang, enemies of Ulli's. They supposed they would be able to catch Ulli, who usually stays out here on his own, and beat him to a pulp. Punishment. Of course, decides Ulli. But in a fair fight. The assaulted sentry takes one of them, Ulli the other. Queensberry rules, natch.

Everyone scoots back against the wall to leave the middle of the room free for a ring. Ulli first. It's soon over, to general regret. A swift punch from Ulli sends his antagonist sprawling on to the empty bottles. One of them breaks on his tough nut. A harmless cut, but blood everywhere. The boy's had enough. He presses his handkerchief against the wound and accepts a half-pint of schnapps from his enemies. The second contest: both lads light into each other like savages. Neither of them has a clue about boxing. They thrash and mill around, clumps of hair fly this way and that, the de rigueur nosebleed. The spectators laugh and joke. The combatants grin wildly with their blood-smeared faces. The whole thing takes a comic turn. Okay, says Ulli, that's enough. It's his birthday, and he's in a mood for forgiveness. The other lad gets given a hefty dose of alcohol as well, then they both mooch off. Everyone knows they won't betray the party. If they did, they are well aware that they would land up in the emergency ward. Betrayal is something that can only be washed clear with blood, and plenty of it.

So on with the party! Bottles do the rounds. One dead soldier after another is tossed into the corner. The gramophone whines away. Whirling chaos, getting louder and louder: alcohol. With frightening speed, the boys on the floor turn into mute quadrupeds. Then someone hurls a word into the chaos: 'Wimmin!' Lust flares up in the boys: yes, women! On the corner of

Kolonie- and Badstrasse there's always an old bird or two. Two lads set out. Return with a woman who won't see forty again. Ulli straightaway sorts out the compensation question by tossing her a ten-mark note: 'For the lot!' Jonny, guest of honour, and boss of an allied gang, makes a start. Then the birthday boy, and after him, everyone, everyone . . . The prostitute lies on a sofa of piled-up potato sacks, smokes one cigarette after another, and takes it in her stride. At the end of an hour, she's earned her ten marks. She has to climb over a knot of boys, lying there lifeless, to get to the door. Silence in the summer house. The altar candle lights a sorry scene . . .

EIGHT

What's going to happen to me, Ludwig asks himself in the chill of prison. And comes up with a prompt answer: a few months' penitentiary for something you didn't do, and then you'll be sent back to the institution. Another three years, basically. What will the Blood Brothers think has happened to him? He has no chance of communicating with them. Not a chink of light anywhere in the grim outlook. He drops on to his bed and stuffs the coarse sheet into his mouth. But he's not able to check his violent sobbing.

The official at the peephole is heartily used to the sight. Eating, drinking, sleeping, answering the call of nature and crying, the whole gamut from silent contained weeping to hysterical wailing. A nice job, allowing the prisoner to beat himself up, by depriving him of the least thing that might take him out of himself, be it no bigger than a fly. That self-recrimination during pre-trial detention spares the investigative magistrate quite a bit of trouble later. The worn-down captive will confess everything and more, just to escape the modern torture of remand and get to face a court.

The following morning Ludwig is told: 'Get ready . . . you're moving to remand prison in Moabit.' Along with a dozen other prisoners, he is pushed into the waiting-pen. The official calls out their names from a list. After each name, he appends the bleak destin-ation: 'Tegel', or 'Plötzensee', or 'Moabit', as he does after Ludwig's name. 'Everyone out!' Into the van that does the rounds of the various prisons. Through a tiny gap, Ludwig is able to see a few inches of Alexanderplatz, and before long they've reached Moabit, their first destination. Policemen accompanying the van deliver the prisoners and their files into the hands of the prison guards. Through the ground-floor office windows, Ludwig is once more afforded a glimpse of free people, speeding cars and ding-a-linging trams. Then there's the stereotypical summons: 'Come along with me.' A glass-roofed and flower-grown passageway connects the office space to the prison itself. The official unlocks the door.

All at once there's no more flowers or friendliness. Prison is grey-on-grey chiaroscuro. Spiralling up into infinity is a system of bare-iron staircases. Floor upon floor. Cell by cell, in a radial pattern, all dominated by the tall watchtower in the middle, where alarm bells go off at the least suspicion. Trusties in blue prison uniforms polish the linoleum floors of the corridors to an even deeper shine. The iron brooms scratch back and forth, back and forth. There's plenty of time here. Many months, if not years. Guards snoop through peepholes at their quarry, lawyers weighed down with files hurry into the consulting rooms to be taken to their clients – their murderers or black marketeers. Little squads of remand prisoners are marched off to the bathroom, to the doctor or to exercise. A prison full of bustle, but the human voice belonging to prisoner number so-and-so is just a shy whisper. Ludwig is taken to reception. Taken everywhere. Here in this well-secured prison, not one prisoner takes a step outside his cell without the law three paces behind him.

'Empty your pockets,' says the guard. Shirt and socks are taken off Ludwig as well. Then a shower of institutional property rains down on Ludwig. Wool blankets, sheets, shirt, socks, handkerchief and neckerchief. Each

62

item carries the stamp of the institution. Next, a shower. 'D'you have lice?' 'No, sir.' The guard stands by as Ludwig reluctantly strips off, and then greedily grabs at his clothes. Turns the pockets inside out, checks the linings, feels the material for any items that might have been sewn in, looks in his boots, searches for contraband: money, knife or rope that might be used in a suicide attempt or flight. And lo, in the corner of a pocket, he finds a little end of string that might do to squeeze a throat shut. It's promptly confiscated and noted, and joins the rest of the impounded stuff. From the shower he goes to the governor. A prison file on Ludwig comes into being. A senior guard takes the new bod to his cell, instructs him in the house rules, on bed-making (very important!) and on keeping his cell clean.

The heavy door clangs shut, Ludwig is on his own. He makes his bed, eyes the three tattered books on the shelf, and sees a few square yards of sunlit sky through the barred window. That's about the size of it for the next few months. And then? A few more, courtesy of the institution. But already Ludwig is certain he will take the first opportunity he gets to run away from the institution. Back to Berlin. He's going to find the wretch who played the trick with the left-luggage ticket on him.

Over the next few days, Ludwig has a couple of meetings with the investigating magistrate. After that, the straightforward case is ready to go to court. Of course the boy stole wallet and luggage ticket at the same time. Take him away, sergeant. Ludwig gets the odd visitor in his cell. The work inspector asks whether Ludwig wants to work or not. Threading glass beads, it's well paid. For ten thousand beads a tad bigger than the head of a pin, the state will pay ten pfennigs . . . so long as the prisoner hasn't lost his marbles after the first five thousand. The prison teacher comes along, and asks about the level of Ludwig's education, what he likes to read, whether he wants to take part in the curriculum. The evangelical minister promises to send along his Catholic colleague, and a representative of the youth department takes lots of notes. The next day Ludwig is taken to the prison doctor: 'Any syphilis or clap?' 'No.' 'Okay, take him away. Next, please. Any syphilis or clap?'

With the mark that cost him so dear, Ludwig buys cigarettes. Fifty at two pfennigs apiece. The smell of the rough tobacco wafts out into the corridor and tickles the nostrils of a desperate trusty. He takes a look round: no guards. He raps quietly on the door of Ludwig's cell, then, with his mouth pressed to the crack, whispers: 'Mate, this is yer trusty. You got 'nything to smoke in there?' Ludwig answers in the affirmative. 'Can you slip me a couple of fags at supper time? So that the guard doesn't see.' Ludwig promises him five cigarettes, and he has an idea. He asks the trusty whether there was any chance he could smuggle a note to the outside. The trusty thinks there is, in the next couple of days some pals of his are being released, they could take a note. But now Ludwig doesn't have a pencil. He says the words through the crack in the door for the trusty to take down. *To Jonny, in Schmidt's pub, on Linienstrasse. Arrested for stealing left-luggage ticket, but I'm innocent! Get me some food and smokes, Ludwig.* The trusty promises, but says: ten cigarettes! Okay. That evening at supper, ten cigarettes are slipped into the trusty's waiting grip.

Three days later. The guard unlocks the door: 'Okay, come with me to the governor, there's a package waiting for you.' Jonny's got the note, it flashes through Ludwig's mind. Right. Before Ludwig's eyes, the governor opens the parcel. On top is a letter, Ludwig recognises Jonny's writing straight away. *Dear Ludwig, I've learned of your misfortune through the Welfare Office, and am sending you food and cigarettes. Thinking of you always, Auntie Elsie. PS Uncle Jonny sends his best.* The governor disregards the harmless note, and carefully checks the contents of the parcel for hidden missives. All he finds though is cake, chocolate, salami, cigarettes, and a bag of sugar. As a remand prisoner, Ludwig is allowed to take it all back to his cell with him. But it's not just the possession of foodstuffs that makes him so deliriously happy. No, it's the fact that Jonny and the other lads outside are thinking of him, and sent a parcel the instant they got his note, the fact that they didn't let him stew once he was gone, that's what makes him so boisterous. Carefully he deposits cake, salami and everything else in the little wall cupboard. And of the hundred cigarettes, he sets ten aside to give the trusty for the prompt execution of his wishes. He means to give him a share of the other things as well, if it's all right with the guard.

He's just picked up the bag of sugar when it splits open, and white sugar rains down into the bottom of the box. Could have been worse. In fact it wasn't bad at all. Ludwig holds the empty bag and gawps inside it. The inside of the paper is covered with writing! Jonny's hand. The bag is a magnificent messenger. Ludwig leans back against the door so that no one can watch him through the peephole. Then he carefully takes apart the bag at the seams. *What happened, old man? What's with this luggage receipt you keep talking about? The note you sent us is completely baffling. What are you in for? For running away from the home? Or was there really some story with a*

66

left-luggage receipt? There's no chance of seeing you, of course. First, we're not relatives, and then it's safer not to, innit? Write again, as before. But not to us, in case the police pick up anything. When the time comes for them to take you back to the home, then make a break for it! We're all expecting you. Jonny, aka Auntie Elsie, and the rest of the Blood Brothers.

Ludwig reads the note till he knows it backwards, then rips up the paper bag and stuffs it down the toilet. The lads! Oh, the lads! And Jonny! My God, that's friendship for you. Thinking of you, even when you're up shit creek. At lunchtime he means to slip the trusty his next batch of cigarettes. Damn! It's someone else. Who knows if he's on the level? No chance of further communications to Jonny.

Three weeks pass in the endless monotony of prison. Then he is sent the charge sheet by the juvenile welfare office. Theft of a wallet; contents: ID in the name of such-and-such, ninety marks in cash, and a left-luggage ticket. Further, falsification of official documents (because he signed his original statement with a false name). In breach of paragraphs — and — . . . A few days later he is summonsed to appear before the juvenile court in Neue Friedrichstrasse. The day before the court date he is told: 'Get yourself ready, you're going back to the police station.' Checks out with the superintendent, returns the prison property. Then back to the convict bus, the pen at police HQ, the reception area, and finally his new cell. The following morning: 'Get yourself ready, you're going to court.'

An underground passage connects HQ with the juvenile court. 'Do you plead guilty to theft?' 'No.' Evidence. Witnesses. The rightful owner of the luggage, the official, the policeman who booked him. A representative of the welfare office is also in attendance. Everything works like clockwork. 'Counsel for the prosecution.' '. . . therefore I argue . . . to be served concurrently, making a sentence of eighteen weeks.' 'Accused?' 'It wasn't me, Your Honour, a stranger gave me . . .' 'Have you anything else to say?' 'No.' 'The court will retire to deliberate.' 'In the name of the people: four months in prison, minus time already served in remand . . . On probation for three years, transferred back to the institution at H. . . . Accused, do you accept the sentence?' Ludwig thinks. If he doesn't, he stays in remand. No, anything to get out, even if it's only back to the home. 'Yes, sir.' 'Final, as of four minutes past eleven.'

Back to HQ, to his cell. Now it's only a matter of time before Ludwig is shipped back to H.

NINE

It's a lovely feeling to lie on a Baltic or Wannsee beach and trickle sun-warmed sand over your naked belly. But on a winter's night, to have only clammy cold sand as pillow, mattress and blanket, is so shocking that even a youth habituated to misery, and escaped from an institution, finds it impossible to linger in such a bed. All the more so when the escapee's name is Willi Kludas and he's just got over a night of terror from Cologne to Berlin. Without having slept a wink, he climbs out of the coffin on Kronprinzen Ufer at 4 a.m. Stands there, doubled over with cold like a gouty old man. There's the Spree, oily and black, Lehrter Bahnhof, the Lessing Theatre. Nowhere a trace of any human activity.

He remembers that the Central Market on Alexanderplatz takes on casual labour at this hour of the morning. Maybe he'll be able to earn a few pfennigs there.

The luxury street Unter den Linden is open to the most desperate of vagabonds, he is even allowed to pass through the central archway of the Brandenburg Gate, if it suits him, the one that was once reserved for the Kaiser. The republic made it possible. No more restrictions. We are all citizens, all enjoy the same rights.

Outside the entrances to the market, the lads are standing around in thick bunches, hoping to be taken on by a trader for an hour or two. The chances are getting slimmer all the time. The traders don't splash their silver around the way they used to. They do the work themselves, they'd rather save their money. Not paying any attention to his fellows, Willi Kludas stands around, not quite believing that he'll be able to land a job. A woman trader calls from the hall: 'Helper . . . over here!' Willi plunges towards her, the whole pack pursuing him. They cluster round the trader. Voices from the pack are raised in menace: 'Wot's he doing here, then? He's not from here . . . taking away our work . . .' An elbow catches Willi in the ribs. 'Get lost, you! 'Spect you've forgotten what it's like, getting a beating?' They shove Willi out of the way. At first, they are successful. Willi is swallowed up in the crowd, the trader has already chosen her man. The horde is still working Willi towards the exit. He is seized by a mad fury. He jumps at one of the youths, and knocks him over. The whole pack howls with fury. Two boys run to the aid of their fellow. Willi lashes out blindly. He can feel blood spurting from his nose. Who cares. His fists smash into the faces of his assailants. The whole despair of the past few nights is discharged in a wild bout of fury.

Suddenly a commotion goes through the watching pack. All of them, including Willi's foes, flee through the hall towards another exit. Willi stands there, panting and wiping his bloodied face. Why have they stopped? Then he sees two market policemen approaching. Damn! Let's get out of here! The nearest stall, with its piles of baskets and boxes, obscures him from the gaze of the police. If they nab you here, you can kiss goodbye to your freedom, Willi my lad. He runs and runs. The well-fed police have long since given up the chase. Willi cleans himself up in the toilets of Alexanderplatz station. The blows, his blood, have made him a little crazy. For a couple of pieces of bread he would knock a man to the floor, if he didn't hand over the bread, say.

It's light. The few who have not yet joined the ranks of the six million starving hurry to their places of work. Don't be late! The boss could be in a bad mood. The businesses, the department stores, throw open their premises, filled to bursting with wares for sale. The staff pull up the shutters outside the window displays; everything looks so seductively wonderful, the watchers feel their mouths watering. But a watering mouth won't satisfy you, just looking won't satisfy you, the smell of food wafting out on to the street won't satisfy you! All that will just enrage the hungry man, make him wilder with the desire to stuff his belly with the excess of the others! Suddenly Willi Kludas is standing in a food emporium. He can't remember how he came to be there. He is standing in front of a glazed construction of sausages and roasts, cheeses and sides of ham, appetisingly arrayed salads and fish. The sales assistant is talking to him. Willi wants . . . A loaf of bread. Yes, start off with a loaf of bread, a whole loaf. Then butter, a quarter-pound, here, and some sausage. Some ham. A tin of Halberstadt sausages, a tin of sardines . . . The sales assistant slices, spatchels the yellow butter into a neat cube, and proceeds to decorate it with one or two slashes.

Willi returns to his senses. What's come over him? These things he's ordering will come to at least five marks. He hasn't got any money! Not a sausage. He calls out to the sales assistant: 'Forgot my wallet . . . back in a jiffy!' and he runs off up the road. Hurries through the endless streets, the grey proletarian streets. With him his hunger, which is getting more and more urgent. Before long, Willi stops in front of another food shop, stares at the displays till everything goes misty before his eyes. Should he go in and beg? Slowly, step by step, he enters a bakery. He's still in the doorway when the rosy-cheeked salesgirl's voice greets him: 'There's no charity here!' They can tell from the look of you, Willi, that you don't have ten pfennigs for rolls.

He crosses the street and marches into a creamery. He is the only customer. At the counter, handily within reach, is a pile of cheap sausage. *Special today, 88 pfg. per pound.* Willi asks for half a pound of butter. The sales assistant turns to the butter tub. Willi grabs a ring of sausage, sucks in his stomach, stuffs the sausage down his trousers, and runs out of the shop. Doesn't hear the cries of the sales assistant, tears round the corner, crosses the road, turns another corner, flies through a labyrinth of streets. Finally he dares to look round. No one is coming after him. No one is watching him. He walks on, the stolen sausage nestling against his empty stomach. On impulse, he jumps up on to a passing bus. When the conductor makes his rounds, Willi jumps off again. Now he can take the chance to eat his sausage.

He gets it out in a doorway. It weighs something in the region of two pounds. That would mean you've stolen sausage to the value of 1.76 marks, Willi! Enough with the thinking now. With his bare hands he tears the sausage in two. He sinks his teeth into meat and fat, chews and grinds the claggy mass. He closes his eyes in animal bliss, snuffling and grunting. A lower-middle-class family of four would make a sausage like that last a week. But a robber, a thief, someone who doesn't need to work for the money, he can get through all two pounds in one go . . . With his belly half full he begins to feel a little anxious about the consequences of the action he perpetrated in a daze of hunger. Already Willi is back to prowling the streets again, wondering where his next meal is coming from. Will he steal something else now? No, never! He'd sooner die, sooner hand himself over to the next policeman. Where will he sleep? One sleepless night hanging under an express, the next one in a sandbox . . . he can't go to a home-less shelter. They ask you for papers. And a hostel charges at least fifty pfennigs a night. He needs fifty pfennigs, that would sort everything out. Then he can turn in somewhere, and after a night's sleep, things won't look quite so hopeless.

Fifty pfennigs. All right. If only he had something he could sell. His anorak? Maybe a Jew would give him fifty pfennigs for it. But now, with the onset of winter, no jacket, no coat? And another night in the open? A third sleepless night? No, there's no two ways

74

about it, he's selling his coat. Please God someone will take it. The first dealer he sees thinks it's a bit worn. 'Try selling it to an unemployed, in the warming hall,' the trader suggests. 'What warming hall?' asks Willi. 'Well, here, the one on the corner of Ackerstrasse and Elsässer Strasse, in the old tram depot, you can't miss it.'

Is there anywhere as bleak as the shelter in the disused tram depot? The clock in the yard tells you all you need to know: for years now it's been stuck at fourteen minutes past one. It hasn't changed from the way it was when the last freezing derelict left it a year ago: grisly in its accumulated filth, its lack of hygiene. Even in the mornings, the place is over-crowded. Beside the entrance there are two or three roughly carpentered benches and tables. At a coffee stall, you can get a pot of coffee for five pfennigs, and two dry rolls for five more. Blind never-washed windows; dust spins up from the stone-flagged floor. Perfect for the tubercular homeless seeking warmth. A short walk to the actual warming hall itself. It's true, it is warm there. Warm to high heaven! The reek of hundreds of unwashed bodies, worn filthy clothes and clouds of cheap tobacco, all stewing in the heat.

The hall is painted in the favourite colours of Berlin welfare organisations: grey-green distemper, with dark-green gloss. Scraped, worn, rubbed away and dirtied by thousands of recumbent backs. A little infirm daylight peeks through the dusty skylight. Placed at intervals in the hall, three or four glowing stoves, long pipes convecting their warmth all over. Along the walls and banked in the centre of the room, leaving aisles at either side, bench after bench. A couple of tacky doors lead to the women's day room and the toilets. That's all. Not the least bit of decoration, not the cheapest splash of colour in the welfare grey-green. Everywhere dirt, grime, rubbish. Signs of years of use, signs of barely masked dilapidation. And in the midst of this desperate lack of cheer, the want of hygiene boosted to thirty centigrade, enjoying this gift from the city of Berlin to its most wretched citizens: hundreds of men and boys. They sit or lie on the benches. They are so tightly packed, you have to row with both arms to get through.

Along the walls are big inscriptions: *Trading Forbidden: No Exceptions.* The aisles are a trading floor, nothing else goes on there but dealing in old clothes. It's a rag market, a bazaar of cast-offs. Every single one of these paupers is set on selling or swapping something with one of the other paupers. Possible things, impossible things, things new and old, are on offer: shoes, socks, shirts, trousers, collars and ties, separate trousers and waistcoats and entire suits, summer coats, winter coats, tunics, ladies' and men's shoes and linens. Tattered books and cheap cigarettes, ghastly sweets and cadged bread. Everything, everything. Not even the human body is off-limits. In the toilets, young fellows offer themselves for twenty pfennigs or a few cigarettes. On the window side that looks out on to the roofed in-yard, a group of men are sitting deliberately away from all the commotion. There are no young men among them. Men of forty and much older. They are all busy doing something. One is sitting there in his oft-patched underwear, jabbing at his trousers with a needle. In fact, several of these men are sewing clothes. An old fellow, bent from long decades of work, is trying to get his clobbered boots into shape. With moving patience, he drills holes in the uppers with a pair of scissors, and sews them up with piano wire. Here people are endlessly playing cards, there they are doing crossword puzzles. There's even a volatile debating society in one corner.

In the aisles, the traders push and jostle. One shouts out: 'A weskit, perfect nick, thirty-five pfennigs!' An interested party stops in front of him. Where is the waistcoat? The trader is still wearing it. The buyer walks round the wearer, scrutinises the waistcoat, finds fault with this and that, and offers twenty-five pfennigs and three cigarettes. The deal goes through. The seller takes off the waistcoat, and buttons up his jacket when he puts it on again. A boy does something similar with his decent shoes. He pulls them off and swaps them for a pair in much worse state and a mark in money. No one is in any way surprised at the exchange. Everyone sees the point of it: a mark means a loaf of bread, and half a pound of marge. Even banking deals are transacted in the warming hall. Someone needs a mark. Someone else is prepared to lend it. As collateral he takes the debtor's unemployment card. The next dole day, tomorrow, they agree to meet in the payments room of the welfare department, and the creditor will keep the debtor in view until he's got his mark back, plus the agreed fifty pfennigs interest.

In the anteroom Willi Kludas takes off his anorak, walks into the day room, and mingles with the traders in the aisle. For a few minutes he takes in how the others go about it, then he calls into the babel of voices: 'One anorak, in perfect state, hardly worn, one mark!' 'One mark for a perfect anorak, one mark, save the price of a coat!' After twenty-odd minutes he's involved in a tough haggle with an interested party. Willi wants his ten groschen, the buyer only wants to pay nine. Furious at so much recalcitrance, the young man slips the jacket on. Unhappily, it's a good fit. 'Well?' 'One mark,' Willi says implacably. A moment ago he'd have been content with half that. 'Well, take your mark, you stubborn git!' Rarely can one mark have been the object of such endlessly happy contemplation. He presses the coin into his palm and stuffs his fist in his trouser pocket. One mark! Fifty pfennigs for kip, twenty pfennigs for ten ciggies? Yes! Ten pfennigs for old leftover rolls? Yes! Which leaves twenty pfennigs for tomorrow. He gets the cigarettes right away from a fellow-trader. Ten for twenty. Throat scratchers, but they produce smoke, taste of tobacco, and make a man content.

The baker on Ackerstrasse, used to custom from the warming hall, hands out eight old rolls and a couple of squashed pieces of cake for his ten pfennigs. 'Thank you, sir,' says a blissful Willi. My God, cake! It makes no difference to your stomach if it's a bit squashed or perfectly preserved. Willi decides to throw down another five pfennigs. At the coffee stall in the shelter, he buys a pot of hot milky coffee. He's had nothing warm since Cologne. Methodically, quite the epicurean, he sits down with a blissful smile at the dirty table, and begins by skimming sausage skins, fag ends and paper scraps on to the ground. Cake demands respect, demands a clean table. He sets down the misshapen, but still tasty, lumps in front of him. They're for last. Dessert. First off, four of the rolls. While his teeth are grinding away at the tough rolls, Willi remembers the stolen sausage. The dough swells in his mouth. Why didn't he think of selling his anorak right away? Then he wouldn't have had to steal. The girl will have got the shock of her life. And now presumably she has to make good the loss out of her own wages . . .

The hot coffee spills down his throat like fire. Oh, that feels so good, to get something warm inside you. And now, now it's the turn of the cake. Wonder when he last had cake? In the institution they gave you stollen on holidays. Two or three slices each. And that didn't taste much different than bread that's been kept next to a bag of sugar. Whereas this here! That's what I call cake! On top there's this soft pinkish yielding stuff. And inside there's even a cream filling. That baker sure is a nice fellow. And all for a few pennies. Now light up, and shuffle into the day room, get a place near one of the hot stoves. Place stays open till three. He's got almost two whole hours just to warm himself.

Willi sits down beside a boy, just a kid really, fifteen or sixteen. The kid looks longingly at Willi's cigarette. Willi registers his look and holds the bag out to the kid. In return, the little fellow feels obliged to tell him about his wretched young life. Even though his mother's in Berlin, he doesn't live with her. He'd sooner hang around the warming hall and spend the night in shelters. How come, Willi asks. The childish lips provide the answer, rough and awful: 'My mum's a whore. She's on the game, and she's gone and let the other room to a couple of other whores. And then they all bring men back to the flat, my mum too . . . And I'm supposed

80

to lie in the alcove behind a curtain while they . . . I preferred to leave . . .' Willi asks if his mother at least supported him financially. 'Oh, she drinks away whatever she makes. She's on the sauce. She's always tippling rum . . . And now she's in hospital. She's got siffylis.' 'Where are you staying tonight then?' Willi asks. 'I'll probably be at Silesian Olga's, she only takes forty pfennigs.' 'Could I stay there as well? I've got nowhere.' 'Sure, course you can.' 'Where can we go when this place shuts?' Willi asks next. 'Oh, we'll go on to the municipal library. That stays open until half past eight, and it's warm. Study, you know. They let you read novels and newspapers, and there's chairs, and it's nice and bright.' At three, when the warming hall closes, Willi heads off with his new friend, who's also called Willi, to the library. To study.

The library in the old stables building has a newspaper-reading room annex, which is open to the general public. In winter, this reading room is so popular that people are regularly turned away. It is pleasantly warm. The tall bright room is full of light and cleanliness. There are newspapers all round the walls. An official sees to it that the character of an afternoon warming hall isn't too painfully obvious. A few taps of a reproachful index finger make the sleeper aware of the unsuitability of his behaviour. The man thus marked blushes in proportion to his sensibility, and immerses himself with fresh enthusiasm in his reading of the serial. Little Willi knows his way around. He pulls down copies of *Simplicissimus* and *Jugend*, and the two of them fall to reading. Willi Kludas has trouble staying awake. He is yearning for the promised mattress at Silesian Olga's.

At quarter to nine on the dot, the librarian tells everyone to hang up their newspapers. A few minutes later the readers, many of them, are standing out on the quiet Breite Strasse, and don't know what to do with themselves. A tormenting night of wandering lies ahead of them. Until seven o'clock, when the warming hall on Ackerstrasse opens its doors to those already waiting.

Silesian Olga has a basement flat in the east of Berlin. She's converted two back rooms into a minimal but inexpensive hostel. If you count the putting out of a few straw sacks as conversion . . . But what more does she need to do for forty pfennigs? Little Willi takes his older namesake into one of the typical stinking backyards that Berlin has by the thousand. The damp reek of mould engulfs them as they walk down the hollowed-out stairs. Silesian Olga is sitting by her stove, patching and sewing at a pair of man's trousers. The trousers of a resident. When else should she mend his things if not now, when the wearer has crawled off to sleep under a filthy blanket?

If a resident can't get together the necessary forty pfennigs, then Olga will still sometimes agree to make an exception. But only if the boy is nice looking . . . Olga's no more than a rattling bag of bones herself. Her willingness to make concessions strikes terror into the hearts of the boys. It's rare that one turns up at the hostel without money, because he knows what's in store for him then . . . 'Evening, boys,' Olga welcomes the two lads, before crawling back to the ruined trousers with her weak eyes. Each of them counts out his due, and is then permitted without further ado to seek out a place for the night. A wretched oil lamp sputters. Mould thrives on a few dirty scraps of wallpaper, and where the straw mattresses are laid out, sharp eyes might make out numerous disgusting bloodstains from squashed bedbugs.

Boys, men and oldsters lie higgledy-piggledy on the floor, sleeping away the wretchedness of their existence. Boys, in whose sleeping mouths milk teeth still shine. Men, whose strong arms would be capable of earning a better billet. Oldsters, whose pathetic weakness would have earned a better billet. Look at the winter garments of that seventy-year-old! His bare feet are in tattered old shoes that are far too big for them. Olga may have declined to patch his trousers. They would be a waste of thread, those rags secured with safety pins and string. Instead of a shirt, the old man wears a disintegrating sweater. On the chest, in racy lettering, is the legend 'Mifa', a make of bicycle. Perhaps a compassionate cyclist gave it to him? He has nothing by way of a jacket, only a coat of ill-defined colour and shape. His long scrawny chicken-neck pokes out of his sweater. His crumpled bird's face looks like it might already have known the grave.

New guests arrive, and flop down silently on straw sacks. Silesian Olga finishes her sewing, lays the items on the sleeper's blanket, and blows out the lights in both rooms. No one will come now. She counts her takings, and puts the money in a saucepan, in a carefully secured hiding place. Slowly Olga starts to take the pins out of her thin chartreuse-coloured hair, and bundles what's left of it into a thin plait. She stuffs a hot-water bottle into the bed beside the basin, the boys all paid up tonight . . . There follows a fantastic production of gaudy petticoats. The bed doesn't even groan as it receives the bony load. Olga remembers something, and starts up again. The lid of the washing cauldron. If one of her sleepers happens to be taken by lust for the money in the saucepan, and sneaks into her kitchen, the lid, balanced on the door, will fall off with an almighty clang and awaken Silesian Olga from her sleep.

TEN

Two days have passed since Ludwig's sentence.
The guard in the remand prison shakes the bell.
A brutal noise shatters the silence of the sleeping
prison. Then the official runs down the corridors: 'Get
up! Get up!' He lets the trusties out first, and then
he opens cell after cell so that they can give the inmates
fresh water. It's the beginning of a new day.

Ludwig is just taking receipt of his can of water
when an official comes along and tells him: 'You, make
ready. At nine o'clock you're out of here.' 'Where to?'
'To H., the young offenders' institution.' Then Ludwig's
on his own again. So it's back to H., is it? Even this

grim news gives Ludwig a bit of encouragement. At last he can leave prison. A ten-hour train ride, away from Berlin, of course, but a change in the weary routine of the last months. Let the chips fall where they may. He won't stay in H., he's sure of that. He quickly dresses, fossicks around with his shoes, brushes and gussies himself up till the trusties come along with their dodgy coffee and a slice of rye bread. The growing boy's constant hunger makes short shrift of the bread, the big strong teeth aren't detained for long. Ludwig sits on the wobbly stool, ready for the off, listening out, like a dog waiting for a walk. He is excited, his cheeks are pink and his eyes bright, as they haven't been in a long while. To think that he'll be outside in half an hour . . . on Alexanderplatz. With the escort, of course. He'll catch a glimpse of Münzstrasse, maybe even the odd acquaintance. Then, suddenly, something crosses his mind: is the escort going to keep him chained up until they're on the train? Because he's not going to stand for that. No way. The key turns in Ludwig's cell door. 'All set?' In the reception area, Ludwig is given back what he had in his pockets when he was admitted. His pencil, his pocket knife, his matches and little notebook. Then he has to sign that everything was properly returned to him. In the pen, he has to stand and wait till the transporter comes for him.

Through an air vent Ludwig hears the surging noise of the Alexanderplatz, the clattering of heels, the oaths of irate drivers, the giggling of gossipy secretaries, and the repeated incomprehensible cries of the newspaper sellers. He can feel his heart beating at his throat, his hands are trembling and slick with sweat. He's almost there, almost. He casts a look at the officials across the partition from him. Calm decent men, sitting at their desks, working through files, files, files. Prison is their career, locking people away is their vocation. They get as much pleasure out of shutting someone up as letting them go again. In or out, what's it to them, they only do what the files tell them.

A little man comes running into the office. Short stout legs in falling down puttees, his rotund belly in a warm tunic. The jolly red face with the never-still pince-nez looks just about as unpolice-like as it's possible to be. He presents his papers, which identify him as the escort of the young offender Ludwig N. Everything is in order, he is presented with the large file, and then he has to sign for it and the associated offender. So far as Berlin is concerned, Ludwig has been dealt with. He is released from the pen, and handed over to the escort. The fat man gives the boy the once-over. 'Well, let's get going, then, shall we. Morning, gents.' He stops down in the yard of the HQ. 'Now, listen to me, Ludwig. My name's Hackelberg, it's my job to take you to the institution at H. We're going to take the underground to Potsdamer Platz, and then we'll walk to Anhalter Bahnhof. I'm supposed to have you on a lead while we're in Berlin' – he shows Ludwig a chain – 'but that's not a nice thing for either of us, is it. So be a sensible lad, and don't get any ideas. If you try and make a break for it at any point, I'll have no option but to have you cuffed. Are we agreed then?' Ludwig answers 'Yes, sir' like a good boy, and looks longingly at the cigar Herr Hackelberg is about to light. 'Fancy a smoke, do you? Well, let's see if we can't buy a couple of cigarettes somewhere,' is the escort's reaction to Ludwig's sheep's eyes.

And now they are walking through the crowds. Herr Hackelberg, seemingly without a care in the world, is drawing on his cigar and giving Ludwig instructions as to his behaviour once they are on the train. Ludwig feels the paving stones under his feet, he feels light-headed like an invalid who's been bedridden for months. All those people, those shops, Tietz's over there, the girls . . . my God, the girls. They've made it to the underground stop in no time, now they go downstairs. Herr Hackelberg buys ten cigarettes at the kiosk. 'There you go, Ludwig, now you can puff away to your heart's content . . .' Ludwig barely manages to blurt out his 'Thank'ee'. Someone being kind to him, giving him cigarettes? It defies belief. Hackelberg is offering him a light before he's dared to open the pack. Then he bursts out with it: 'Thank you . . . oh, thank you so much, Herr Hackelberg. No one's shown me any kindness for such a long time . . .' How long is it since he last smoked? The last cigarettes he had were the ones Jonny sent. He gulps, swallows the smoke and blows it out in dense clouds.

Now here's their train. In spite of the crowd, Herr Hackelberg is adept at keeping Ludwig at his side at all times. He's also given him his file and his little suitcase to carry. The boy would have to fling those away if he made a dash for it, and by the time he does I'll have got him again, he thinks. They have to change at Friedrichstadt. The crowds in these underground-transfer stations are something to behold. Everyone walking, running, jogging into each other and past each other. Your Berliner hates to miss a train. That would mean having to wait two minutes till the next one! Even a jobless man will leap aboard a moving train. It must be an old instinct, dating back to the time he was still gainfully employed . . .

Ludwig, with case and file, twists his way through the crowds. By his side is the alert Hackelberg. They have to go down a long passage called Consumption Corridor. Two young men are barging their way through the other passengers, to catch the train pulling in at the far end of the passage. 'For Chrissakes, get a move on, won't you! Get on with it,' calls one, then they disappear into the mass. 'For Chrissakes get a move on.' The words echo in Ludwig, bring him to life: git on wiv it! He can feel it whispering to him, exhorting him: run, break, do one! He's forgotten his earlier gratitude for the ten cigarettes. A new feeling, his hunger for freedom, swills away all that.

Crash! The case and file are down at Herr Hackelberg's feet, impeding him. Ludwig clears a path for himself with fists and elbows, races down the steps into the tunnel. Parts the human seas with both arms, squeezes, twists, forces himself through every little gap, hugs the wall, where there's liable to be the most space. No one is surprised at the boy's hurry, they're just furious at the way he's knocked them aside and trodden on their shoes. Ludwig can hear a roaring inside him: For Chrissakes, get a move on . . . run . . . or else he'll catch you! At the same time, he's thinking urgently: where to? If there's a train at the platform, jump on board. Otherwise, up to street level and on to a passing bus. The platform. A train is just pulling out, it's already putting on speed. Pull at the door, run alongside . . . jump! Helping hands pull him into the carriage. Panting hard, he stands among the passengers. The train races west. If a ticket inspector happens by, Ludwig, you're out of luck.

What about Herr Hackelberg? He did his best. Left everything lying there, set off in pursuit and yelled his 'Stop! Stop!' It was his bad luck that a train was just leaving. The stationmaster assumed his 'Stop!' was for the train, and thought Herr Hackelberg meant to jump on to it. As duty obliged him, he held him back. Held on to him. And before Herr Hackelberg, distressed as one may imagine, was able to explain the situation to him, Ludwig was gone. Only the case and file could still be retrieved. So back to HQ. He wasn't to blame for any of it. It said expressly on the transport papers: *Cuffing not essential.*

Ludwig rides for three stops. Then he transfers to another line. Changes again. Always stands by the door so that, if an inspector should come, he can get out right away. What now? Back to the gang! You don't stand a chance alone in Berlin. He doesn't have a penny. He won't risk the vicinity of Münzstrasse, where the Blood Brothers hang out, not so close to police HQ. But how is he to contact Jonny or one of the others? He could try calling Schmidt's, at this time of day there's bound to be a Brother there. But then he doesn't have a coin for the phone! The train is really flying now. Ludwig can't even make out the names of the stations. Where's he going to get a coin from? On the opposite seat is a thrown-away paper from today. New, barely looks opened. Ludwig picks it up. The twelve o'clock edition of the *B. Z.* He has an idea. The train is stopping, not before time. Gesundbrunnen station. He quickly gets out. Climbs up to Brunnenstrasse. Heads in the direction of Badstrasse. Looks at the clock, at the newspaper kiosks. No, it's not here yet. Up here, in the far north of Berlin, it doesn't usually get here before half past twelve.

Once again, Ludwig takes a look around in all directions. Policemen? Nope. He chances it. He calls out: '*B. Z.* – noon edition!' and waves the paper in front of him. He shouts four times, and then he's shot of it, and he's got a coin for the phone. Back to Gesundbrunnen station, to the call box. He knows the number by heart. Even before anyone says hello, he can hear the oom-pah-pah music. His face cracks in a smile. The old days at Schmidt's. Then a voice, Jonny's, in person. He listens. Doesn't ask many questions. Only: where are you? And: where can we meet, I'll grab a taxi. Ludwig suggests the Vinegar Cinema. Jonny knows. He'll be there in no more than fifteen minutes. See ya.

Vinegar Cinema? On the corner of Brunnen and Volta is a big vinegar factory. The whole area has the biting reek of vinegar. People here keep their lips pressed together when they go by on the pavement. The smell makes his mouth water. There is a cinema next to the factory, so what else are they going to call it? It's the Vinegar Cinema.

Still feeling very uncertain, Ludwig walks into a doorway and watches from there to see if a taxi draws up in front of the cinema. There it is, and it's Jonny. He looks around. Ludwig charges across the street. 'Hey, Jonny!' He can't repress his joy; a few tears, wiped away with the back of his hand, spurt from his eyes. There's no one better than Jonny in a situation like this. He firmly shakes Ludwig by the hand, and steers him into a bar. A small instant calmative, then Ludwig can tell him all about it in some quiet café. After a beer and a short, Ludwig calms down. They walk to a small café. They are the only customers in the back room, and Ludwig has the floor. First there's an excellent brew, and a torte with whipped cream. Things that haven't been part of Ludwig's world for a long time. He talks. Starts off with the fellow outside Stettiner Bahnhof. 'We'll put a crimp in his style,' says Jonny.

At the end of half an hour, Jonny is fully up to speed. For the next few days, things will be a bit ticklish for Ludwig. He will have the police looking for him. And if he is caught, then that'll be the end of his probation and he'll have to do four months.

93

But the long-term outlook isn't bad. He's not a serious criminal. And no fewer than five gang members feature on the police wanted list, just because they fled borstals. The authorities would have their work cut out if they were going to chase after every runaway youth. So long as he doesn't rub it in . . .

ELEVEN

At 7 a.m. Willi Kludas is woken by his little name-sake. 'Hey, Willi, there's been a blizzard. Come on, we'll go with the street cleaners, there's always help taken on when it's snowed.' In no time Willi is alert. As he gets dressed, he chokes down a couple of the leftover rolls from yesterday, and gives his little friend the last two. In the kitchen they hold their heads under the cold tap; Silesian Olga even has a rag for them to dry their heads on. Hurry, hurry, says little Willi. Jacket on, collar up, and cap. In the court-yard, the little fellow suddenly stops in the slush. 'Have you got any papers, you need to show them.'

Papers? Forget it, Willi Kludas. They don't issue you with papers in the institution when you do a runner. Then I'm not going neither, the little fellow wants to say, out of solidarity, when all at once he gets an idea.

He can hardly speak for excitement, and it takes him a while to when he finally can. 'You've still got twenty pfennigs, ain't you? We'll go out and buy a broom handle with that, and they'll give us the side of a tea chest for nothing . . . Then we'll rig up a snow shovel at Olga's, and I know she's got a broom too, an ancient thing. And then we'll go round the shops. "Morning. Your bit of pavement looks parlous. Don't think your customers will be willing to risk their necks on that. But if you like, we can get it cleaned up for you, nice and cheap . . ." And I bet we'll have earned us a couple of marks by afternoon. Isn't that a good idea?' They dash into the nearest soap shop. A broom handle costs fifteen pfennigs, and they are able to pick up the lid of a box of soaps for nothing. Silesian Olga is flattered and cajoled till she coughs up her old broom and a few nails. The snow shovel is put together in no time, and the two Willis rush off.

To Breslauer Strasse. Their timing is perfect. The shopkeepers are just opening their stores, and, half-asleep still, are staring at the night's slushy gift. Third time lucky. A bony little confectioneress biddy. Willi

Kludas gives the pusher its initiation, the little man scratching after with the broom, and asks in the shop for some ashes to strew. At the end of half an hour, the snow is cleared away, and the biddy pays them each thirty pfennigs, and a bag of sweet leftovers. They're in the black. They threw in the dairy basement next door. Just a few yards, but it's thirty pfennigs between the two of them. Across the road, the big dry-cleaning business is too cheap to spare any change, they've sent their pallid girl trainee out on the street. Keep going, Willi. Here a nibble, there none. Here has been cleaned already, there they're kept talking till they're blue in the face, over a few pfennigs.

At the end of five hours, the boys are way up on Frankfurter Allee, and things are getting stickier. Clean pavements as far as the eye can see. 'Call it a day, Willi?' 'I think so too, Willi.' They stop for dinner in a cheap restaurant. Three courses, with soup and a wedge of pudding. Then they do the accounts. Even after paying for dinner, they each have four marks and change. Willi Kludas hasn't had this much money since forever. They park their tools at Silesian Olga's. Who knows, maybe it'll snow again tonight. Olga is delighted with a paper twist of sweets, and here are twice forty pfennigs for the night ahead.

My God, doesn't Berlin look different when there's something in your pockets that jingles! Even if it's

97

only four marks. Willi Kludas walks through the streets at the side of his friend, with a luminous grin on his face. Their bellies are full, they have cigarettes in their pockets, they have paid for the night, and they're in the money. 'Say, what do you think about going to the cinema?' asks the younger Willi. 'Pritzkow's only costs forty pfennigs.' The Pritzkow cinema on Münzstrasse is not just a cinema where they show Westerns and cop shows. It also serves as a warming hall and a dormitory for those sufficiently flush to be able to afford the entrance money. For forty pfennigs, anyone is entitled to a seat from ten in the morning till eleven at night. There he can watch the show six times over or else sleep through it, he can take his pick. In the terms used by the regulars, you don't pay entrance money just so that you walk out again two hours later. At Pritzkow's you pay sleeping money, and you hang around accordingly. The narrow little cinema is jam-packed at all hours. The boys and youths sit pressed together, some staring with fascination, some in stupor at the cacophonous screen, or they're already making back their sleeping money. Gently slumped on the seat in front or the neighbour's shoulder, or with sagging head counting their waistcoat buttons.

Willi Kludas stares at the screen open-mouthed. For him this modest production is something of a miracle.

He had no idea there was such a thing as sound films, and those girls up on the screen . . . they're so bonny . . . and the way everything jiggles on them when they walk . . . The way they throw themselves at the well-dressed gentlemen and snog them . . . phwoar! And their sweet singing voices . . . and how they flip their skirts in the air when they dance. Willi Kludas shifts around on his chair, his face is burning and his sweaty fingers are tying knots. To get a girl like that . . . to watch a girl . . . In the interval he asks his little name-sake if he had ever seen a girl in the altogether. He himself hadn't, not properly. Where could he have? At sixteen he was put in the borstal. Someone there had had a lot of pictures of fat naked women. This boy loaned the cards out to his friends at night. In return for cigarettes, or a piece of sausage, or the meat ration at dinner. Then the boys would go up to the window to get a proper look at the cards. For half an hour at a time they would stand there gawping at the naked photographs, and then in bed afterwards . . . well, what else was a boy going to do? And then there was Otto Kellermann, a lad with golden hair and pale skin like a girl's, who called himself Ottilie, and if you wanted your turn with Ottilie you had to pay as well . . .

Little Willi's experience was vastly different. His teenage years were poisoned by his own mother, who gave herself to strangers in the room where he slept.

By the tenants who brought their johns into the room, and sometimes drunkenly staggered up to Willi's bed: 'Willi, darling, aren't you old enough yet . . . do you fancy it, then . . . keep still, sweetheart . . .' The mystery into which the twenty-year-old Willi Kludas was inducted with the help of smutty pictures and his friends' obscene speeches had been revealed to little Willi at thirteen under still more profane circumstances.

They leave the cinema and head back out onto Münzstrasse. Willi Kludas stares under every tart's hat brim, and if he's accosted with a practised smile and a swaggering display of breasts and bum, then he feels a lustful itching that burns through him, dries his throat and makes his legs tremble. His damp hands in his trouser pockets clutch his money . . . Enough to have one of those girls. But he's ashamed in front of his comrade. It would be a different matter if he was on his own . . . 'What'll we do now?' asks the boy. 'Do you know anywhere where there are lots of girls?' is Willi's counter-question. 'The fairground?' proposes the boy. 'Are there any there?' 'Christ, any number . . . behind the toilets for fifty pfennigs,' comes the expert answer.

The Silesian Fair on Schillingbrücke. Pleasure garden for all the gangs in the east of Berlin. Scene of daily jealous battles over a squeeze. Berlin's nastiest red-light area; schoolgirls, and girls just out of school. Price: five rides at the funfair, a trip to the Hippodrome, ice lollies or potato pancakes, according to season. The more advanced of the child prostitutes have graduated to cash money. Scene of the transaction: behind the toilets. Cap cheekily shoved back so that the hair spills out over their eyes, cigarettes in the corners of their mouths, men between fourteen and twenty take in the daily parade of women between twelve and eighteen. Glances, and sometimes more than glances, assess bodies whose owners reciprocate by trying to show them off to best advantage.

Outside the funfair there's Elly, a pretty, well-made thing of sixteen, staring yearningly at the whooshing swing boats. Little Willi knows her. 'Do you fancy her then?' he asks Willi Kludas. The acquaintance is soon made. Willi buys tickets for three rides, and piles into a boat with Elly. Pulls on the strap so hard that after a few swings it's touching the top of the frame and the operator has to use all his strength to brake. With coquettish fear Elly sits clasping Willi's legs. Another ride, and another, and then they find themselves back on solid ground again. Elly stretches, smooths her dishevelled hair, and lets the impressionable Willi into a few secrets about her build. He's a cute boy, and not half strong . . .

A boy who knows what he owes his new bride is

duty bound to treat her to potato pancakes. Little Willi does the honours on behalf of his gormless elder. After potato pancakes, Willi Kludas and Elly are sitting in a little dodgem car on the Iron Lake. Round the corners, Elly shows her expertise at pressing her soft body against his. Willi staggers out of the car like a drunk, and clutches Elly's arm. Where did the little fellow get to then? Just as well he's gone. We'll meet up at Olga's later anyway. Elly is in the mood for a drink. Where, asks Willi. They go to the Whale, opposite the fairground.

It's a big beer bar where the garlands hang every day from 1 January to 31 December. The band, with trumpet and drums at the fore, is evidently under strict and simple instructions to bend their efforts to the making of as much noise as possible. And lo, they succeed, for dear life if nothing else. Because the customers' idea of entertainment in the overcrowded bar is a drunken shouting and rampaging around. Narrow passages between tables have long since been taken up by scraping shifting chairs. The whole bar is a seething confusion, swathed in the smoke of mostly non-export-quality cigarettes. In the midst of it all, scouts in a desperate pickle, are the waiters. On each one of ten fingers, defying gravity, a beer. Jammed against each elbow, if possible, oval plates with vast helpings of pork and sauerkraut.

The band comes to an understanding that they need to give their instruments a rest if they are to go on playing until closing time, and the drummer is given a signal to end. He obliges with an extra-powerful cymbal crash. For a second or two there is the grotesque auditory spectacle of a wildly yelling mob, whose vocal cords were until recently in an implacable struggle with the band. Then, seemingly abashed by its yelling, the whole bar is suddenly shtum. In that second of silence, a girl's voice is heard, squeaky, loud, but appealing, calling: cigars, cigarettes, chocolates! The cigarette girl. Willi waves her over. Cigarettes for himself, a bar of chocolate for Elly. Then the waiter brings them their pints. By the time Willi has paid, he has exactly twenty pfennigs left. What does he care? Elly has slipped off her coat and is showing herself off to her boy in a skimpy red dress that proclaims all the amenities of her body in stentorian tones. She is aware of Willi's staring burning eyes, and moves in a little closer. By now the band, refreshed by a round or two of free beers, is striking up again. The customers too are back to shouting in one another's faces, apparently delighted at the healthy state of their voices.

At eleven o'clock, Willi walks Elly home. Elly has her own place; the family she does for occupies a ground-floor apartment, and Elly has a little room at the back. With heart beating wildly, Willi stands in the unlit yard, waiting for a ground-floor window to open somewhere. A few minutes later, he is sitting in Elly's room. They aren't able to talk much. Yes, the family live at the front, but . . . Willi sits there, stiff and mute. Timidity, panic, lust for the girl spin round and round, chasing each other within him. He watches Elly get undressed. Two round white arms emerge from the red dress. A subtle, wholly bewildering smell of young female flesh billows around him, causing him to moan quietly. Elly plonks herself down on the bed and takes off her last layers under the sheets. When at last her soft nakedness presses herself against his body, and she squeezes his glowing face between her almost-maternal breasts, then the accumulated sexual deprivation of years of welfare institutions is discharged with almost-animal roars.

Two hours later, exuberant as a little boy, Willi is strolling through quiet night-time streets. The great experience is singing and whooping inside him. The great experience he has heard cheapened, thousands of times, in the tales of his friends. The great natural experience that welfare kept from him for so long. The great experience he pictured for himself in garish fevered colours, during tormented sleepless nights. The great sublime experience in the arms of tubby little Elly . . .

Willi is in luck. He's spent all his money on Elly, but in the morning little Willi is shaking him: 'Oi, get up, it's snowed again!' Snow? That means he can earn money again! Off with snow shovel and broom. As they work, little Willi asks how the evening went. But Willi only gives evasive answers. Something as lovely as that you need to keep under your hat. Oh, Elly . . . The shovel works like a dream, it's all the broom can do to keep up. And by the afternoon, they've earned another ten marks.

Three days later. No further snowfall, alas, and Willi is trying to make his bit of money last. In the morning he wakes up feeling terrible. Everything hurts. What's the matter with him? When he tells little Willi, he breaks into a grin, and asks: 'Did you look and check?' Check . . . check what? 'I expect you will have gone to bed with Elly.' Before long, the little boy has diagnosed that Willi's got a dose of the clap. Elly infected him. 'You need to get yourself seen by the doctor right away, and you'll be fine in two weeks.' 'Doctor? I've got no money, and no papers.' 'You don't need them, Willi, you get seen to for nothing.'

In the late afternoon, the boy takes him to a big building in Köllnischer Park. The doorman gives them a number, and tells them to wait in the back building. In a room, there are up to a hundred boys and men, sheepish or shit-eating grins on their faces. Lads from sixteen to twenty make up the majority. When Willi's number is called, a nurse leads him to an office, where a case register is started for him. 'What name shall I put down?' Willi hesitates. 'I don't want your actual details, I just need a name to put on the file,' the official says. 'Okay, Schröder,' says Willi. He is given a little grey card: *State Insurance: Berlin. Medical department C., for Herr Sch.*, and is taken to a huge white room that is divided up into separate treatment areas by moveable partitions. In every cell is a desk, an examination chair and other medical equipment.

A doctor inspects Willi. 'Where did you get your infection?' Willi is silent. 'Are you able to identify the party so that we can have them taken to a doctor?' What's he going to say, is he going to betray Elly? No, he'll send her along in person. 'I don't know the girl's name . . . we met at the fairgrounds . . . don't know her address neither.' *MP – name and address of suspected party unknown*, the doctor writes on the patient sheet under the rubric 'source of infection'. 'MP' stands for multiple partners. The abbreviation tends to be used with persons suspected of being involved in prostitution. The doctor calls a nurse into the room: 'Would you take a blood sample, just in case.' The blood taken from Willi's left arm will be sent to a laboratory and subjected to a Wassermann

106

test. In three days, Willi will be told whether, in addition to gonorrhoea, he has been given syphilis by Elly as a memento.

Along with the transfer note for a treatment centre, Willi is given a little booklet on sexually transmitted diseases. It contains the endlessly sagacious sentence: *The only dependable protection from sexually transmitted diseases is the avoidance of all sexual activity before marriage.*

TWELVE

During Ludwig's time in chokey, lots of things have changed in the gang. All the boys have got new clothes. A few, Fred, Jonny and Hans, have new wardrobes from head to toe, with good suits and even winter coats. There's money sloshing around as well. Jonny straight away organises a collection for Ludwig among the Brothers. 'To help him forget his time inside.' Ludwig is presented with forty-two marks. He is to buy himself a coat with the money, and various bits and pieces he needs. On the evening of the day Ludwig made his successful break for freedom, there is a big pub crawl in his honour. All the boys are really glad to have him back. And the fact that he ran away so fearlessly in an underground station, that lifts him up a peg or two in everyone's eyes. While the geezer who gave Ludwig the stolen luggage chit, he'd better count his bones if they ever catch up with him. The meanness. When he could have just gone up to him and said: 'Hey, this is a stolen ticket. Do you want to pick up the suitcase? We'll go fifty-fifty.' That would have been appropriate, but this . . . He'd better watch it!

Ludwig is worried about showing up at so many bars in one night. It would just take one little raid in one of them and he's in shtook, seeing as he's got no papers. Papers, papers . . . Jonny muses. Then: 'Come with me.' They head over to Grenadierstrasse, Berlin's ghetto, the street of the little illicit businesses and dives. Jonny exchanges a few words with an old Jewess standing by a cellar opening. She calls a boy up out of the cellar and sends him off on an errand. After a few minutes, he returns with a little wrinkled-looking Jew in a greasy kaftan. The old man's beard and hair are a greenish tangle, his small eyes peer restlessly this way and that. The Jew takes Jonny and Ludwig into his shop.

The term 'shop' is a wild exaggeration. You could purchase its entire stock and have change from ten marks. A few venerable biscuits, the inevitable garlic, a few packets of kosher margarine. The shop is just a blind anyway, a mask for other, better lines of business that don't need stock. They go into a dark windowless back room. The Jew sits down between Ludwig and Jonny on an erstwhile sofa. Devout, submissive and innocent, the old fence folds his black-veined hands together. 'What are the gentlemen looking for?' 'My friend here needs papers,' begins Jonny. 'Papers . . . oh . . .' Straight away, the old man becomes suspicious and reserved. False papers are a difficult business. Jonny is offering fifteen marks for a police registration certificate or an unemployment card. The old man's fingers are playing nervously with his kaftan, fear and cupidity are in equipoise. No, he doesn't do papers. He is an honest man. Yes . . . But . . . he knows someone who does do that sort of business. 'What are we waiting for, then? Let's go see him,' Jonny interrupts.

The someone turns out to be an ancient wizened old woman on the fourth floor of a back apartment. First off, the old man has a big powwow with the little lady. A grisly mix of Yiddish, Hebrew, and German. Then the old man explains to Jonny and Ludwig in a lachrymose sing-song that someone had lived here, he was registered with the police and everything was in order. But one day he hadn't come home, and had thus cheated the honest old lady out of her rent money. The only things he had left behind were

110

a soiled shirt and a bunch of papers in a cigar box, including police registration, his tax card and a baptismal certificate. 'Let's see 'em,' says Jonny. The registration is made out for the flat on Grenadierstrasse, and is in the name of August Kaiweit from Königsberg, born in 1908. Now, Ludwig was born in 1912, and as a native of Dortmund he has barely heard of Königsberg, but in general the papers are not bad. 'Where did the man live?' Jonny asks. The old lady takes him to a wretched closet. 'Rent?' 'Five marks a week.' 'And the papers?' Once again, the two old people fall into an endless back-and-forth, incomprehensible to Jonny and Ludwig. Result: ten marks for the papers, and five marks commission for the old Jew.

Done. Jonny gives the old lady ten marks for the papers, and five marks' rent down on the first week; the Jew is paid his commission. Ludwig has got himself a new name and new digs, in one fell swoop. Now, August Kaiweit need have no fear of police raids. Admittedly, the papers wouldn't work at police HQ, where they've got Ludwig's prints and photographs on file. Moreover, it's not impossible that the real August Kaiweit has a police record and is on some wanted list somewhere. Perhaps he's even a crook; in view of these dodgy Grenadierstrasse digs, that's even quite likely. But there it is: if Ludwig was risk averse, then he might as well hand himself over to the police. A life outside the law is not the same as shelter in the bosom of Abraham . . .

He takes the front-door key from the old lady, and leaves with Jonny. On Münzstrasse there is the parting of ways. Ludwig to look for an old coat from a dealer, and Jonny . . . Jonny has something to go to that involves Fred. Them and their secrets, thinks Ludwig. Rendezvous: eight o'clock at the Rehkeller on Prenzlauer Strasse, just up from Alexanderplatz.

Alexanderplatz! The focal point of Berlin's underworld. Familiar – who hasn't seen the movies? The aristocratic gangsters, who won't do a job except in top and tails. Those sinisterly beautiful evil-doers, for whom murder is a perverse hobby. And the beautifully realistic criminal cellars with Apache dancers, Brylcreemed villains, classy two-mark whores with fire-red mops of curls. The discreet champagne lounges in the basements, and the trapdoors. All provided by the glib and deficient imaginations of directors and other second-raters. The amusement industry clamours for the like. It wants cheap thrills for its expensive balcony seats. So the criminal underworld's the thing. And because the social misery of the actual underworld is not the kind of thing Kurfürstendamm pays money to see, Berlin is given a fictitious one instead, one which, as above, lives in the lap of luxury. The superficial observer of this falsified milieu would find Berlin's actual criminal underworld deathly dull. Nothing of interest there, nothing. Blood is a precious liquid, here as there, and Berlin's villains go to admire the demonic super-criminal in the same place as everyone else – the cinema. It needs closer study to get through to those people who, between brief spans at large, measure out their lives in long prison sentences, in constant flight from the law, and – after a few days of joy, vegetate in ever-deeper deprivation.

Their own choice? Not always, by no means! A youth spent in welfare, more or less apprenticed to crime, that isn't a self-chosen destiny. And then: prior convictions! Untold numbers fail at the difficult glass-hard wall of bourgeois prejudice and desire for retribution. Untold numbers who might have liked to try a law-abiding life for a change.

First: the realisation that the criminal basements as they are shown to us in scores of films no longer exist in Berlin today. All those basements on Linienstrasse, Marienstrasse, Auguststrasse, Joachimstrasse, Borsigstrasse and so on, they were forced out of business after the inflation. And the big beer joints with their lively oom-pah-pah music from early morning on, they are just waiting rooms for armies of pimps, unemployed and casual criminals. But a clientele like that isn't enough to keep a place in business. What keeps these places going is prostitution. It alone keeps them going. It gets the johns in, and drives them to big bar-tabs. Unattached prostitutes aren't great consumers of anything, they wander from table to table offering themselves, or cadging a drink from a guest who's there for a thrill. And when there *is* something really happening in those places, then you may take it for granted that it's all a set-up, so that the voyeurs order another round, and tell their friends about this amazing underworld bar.

The stage set took up the underworld theme, dished up a hundred per cent tall tales, and now the underworld itself is turning into the stage set, so as not to prove too much of a disappointment. It even advertises in the commercial section of the press. Between ads for feudal eateries and worldly *palais de danse*, you see the shout: '*Interested in experiencing the Berlin underworld? Try Europe's best-known restaurant on Alexanderplatz!*' Does it matter that the best-known restaurant in Europe is just a pick-up joint? The underworld is in quotation marks. So much the better for the metropolis, if that was the full extent of its underworld. Alas, it's too good to be true.

Alexanderplatz in the hours between 9 p.m. and midnight. Where to start in the confusion of humanity? Prostitution in every form. From the fifteen-year-old girl, just slipped out of welfare, to the sixty-year-old dreadnought, everyone is feverishly on the make. Male prostitutes, flocks of them, outside the toilets, in bus and tram stops, outside the big bars. Homeless of both sexes sniff around. Loiter, move off. Aimlessly. Sit on a pile of planks for the new underground station. 'Move along now!' Police patrol. Move along, sure, where to? It's almost tempting, the looming bulk of the police HQ on Alexanderplatz. There you can get something to eat and drink and a bed for the night. But only if the desperate fellow has hurled a brick through a shop window.

Pimping, with its specific grimness, is everywhere. Hundreds on Alexanderplatz alone. They own the street, and they certainly own the working girls. They stick to the punters like glue; yes, they animate flagging interest by talking up the girls. Human beings are touted and appraised like lame nags in a horse market.

A swarm of rowdy fun-seekers spills out of an underground beer joint next to the UFA cinema. Straight away, the traffic is brought to a standstill. The crowd is milling around, growing all the time. At the core of the disturbance are a prostitute and her pimp. He is laying into the woman with both fists. She is standing doubled over, her hands protectively in front of her face. She looks like a beast in a slaughterhouse. From the crowd come enthusiastic shouts: 'That's right, Fritz, give it to her!' And Fritz doesn't stint, he gives it to her all right. Not a finger, not a voice is raised on behalf of the woman. Surely, he is among friends here. If the woman gets a beating, she will have deserved it. Finally, the police turn up, clear a way through the surly wall. What happens? Nothing. The pimp has his papers on him, the victim is his wife. And the wife, when invited to by the police, declines to bring charges. She doesn't want to be beaten to a pulp later on by her pimp husband's close friends. 'It looks worse than it is,' is all she says, the blood streaming from her nose.

The huddle of people breaks up. No more trouble. Interest is gone. The prostitute stands at a bus stop, sobbing and dabbing at her nose. 'Now, that's enough of that, Edith.' The pimp, perfectly amiable. And Edith tries desperately to shut up, but the occasional sob still shakes her. She pulls out lipstick and powder, to try and restore order to her teary face. Then they go, arm in arm, to the nearby Rehkeller.

It's the only one of the so-called cellars to deserve the ascription of criminal dive. But even here everything is lite. Underworld is a style. A low arched room with dim-coloured lights. The ancient oft-painted walls give off an appalling reek of mould. A pianist makes despairing efforts to bang out a coherent sequence of notes from a tangle of wire in front of him. Clientele: the usual Alex mob, admittedly with very

116

few tourists. Doesn't promise much from the outside, the Rehkeller.

The Blood Brothers are sitting at a table in the deepest darkest corner of the bar. Sitting with them is a girl of seventeen or eighteen. Anneliese, the new sweetheart of the Brothers. Anneliese has come into the gang ever since, in some way still unknown to Ludwig, they have come into money. Ludwig shows up in his new coat. Anneliese welcomes him with a great smacking kiss. They have never met before, and Jonny explains to Ludwig that Anneliese is part of the gang. The other Brothers greet Ludwig with a facetious, 'Evening, Herr Kaiweit.' Ludwig is flavour of the month. Anneliese sits on the lap of the 'poor lad who was innocent and did time in Moabit', and comforts him at any opportunity with kisses and petting. The first round of schnapps is brought, and they all solemnly intone: 'Here's to you, Ludwig.' Then he has to tell them all about it. How he was nabbed, the interrogation, his time in the Alex, the juvenile court hearing, the moment he spotted Auntie Elsie's secret message to him on the inside of the sugar bag. What the food was like inside, how they treated him, and in minute detail, how he did his bunk in Friedrichstadt station. The escort seemed to be a decent enough fellow, but freedom is freedom. The gang are ever so proud of their Ludwig when he tells them about picking up the discarded copy of the *B. Z.* on the train, and how that helped him get the money to make a call. My God, what a sharp lad! 'Cheers! August Kaiweit!' And Jonny adds: 'And here's to us collaring the evil-doer who tricked you in the first place.'

The pianist announces a rumba, and knocks out something that might equally well be a tango or a black bottom. The girls go looking for a few feet of space to dance with their sweethearts, and Anneliese grabs hold of Ludwig, who now has to go and rumba. This time yesterday he was still lying on a pallet in police detention, with the evening's flour soup glugging in his belly, and the guards' hobnailed boots clanking about in the corridor. 'Kiss me, Anneliese,' he manages to whisper.

The bill is paid. The Blood Brothers move off. Where to now? What about the Mexiko? 'Not there again,' replies Fred, grinning. The Alexander Quelle on Münzstrasse is an unappetising place, but always packed. The din of the brass music is enough to blow the head off your pints, and the mass-produced tobacco smoke keeps the paper chains in a constant spin. Gang members of all ages, abjectest prostitution, layabouts, male and female beggars. They are, all of them, responsible for polishing the pate of the land-lord, who can no longer stand to breathe the fug of his joint and stands outside the door. It is unbelievably full. The newest latecomer has to squeeze inside the door and yell for his beer or schnapps or whatever he wants. The gang barge their way through; of course there's no space anywhere. Right at the back, in front of the upstairs toilets, they manage to huddle round a couple of already-occupied tables. They don't mind being squashed together.

Ludwig, Anneliese, Jonny and Fred are sitting between skeletal looking dossers, come to try and forget the chicken ladder of their lives with a *Koks* or a *Korn* with a dot (*Koks*: rum with a piece of sugar; *Korn* with a dot: kummel with a drop of raspberry). Jonny orders a round of *Koks*. The dossers included, of course. An old geezer with a long white beard is finishing his supper. In his left hand he has a half-wrapped sausage end, from which he slices piece after piece with the paring knife in his right, and pops them into his mouth with bread. The ancient face with the sprouting white hair looks like a throwback to those bygone films where the good child by the garden fence throws a coin into the nice old man's hat. 'Well, Grandpa, aren't you going home yet?' asks Fred. 'Home?' The oldster looks up quickly, before returning to his end of sausage. Then: 'The manager's going to throw me out, I already owe him for four nights. I've reached my limit, so he says.'

119

Calm, objective, quite convinced that the manager is well within his rights, the words come out interrupted by the gummy chewing of his food. The heat in the bar is such that sweat is pouring down the creases of his face. Still the old man won't be induced to take off his coat. Probably he doesn't have a jacket on underneath. He takes his hat off. His snow-white hair curls over his collar and ears. The coppery face has the eyes of a beaten dog. A second schnapps and a cigar give the beggar a little self-confidence. 'Where you from, old man?' He's been out west, around Wittenbergplatz, begging. Up and down backstairs. Since nine o'clock this morning. And all the fine gentry in that area, their contribution to his welfare totalled seventy-two pfennigs, a couple of crusts of bread, and – the old man shows them off proudly – a pair of glacé gloves that are too much of a pair: in fact, they are two right hands.

As he tells his story, a trace of something resembling indignation comes into his voice: 'Four flights up, I'm knocking on the kitchen door. A servant is about to give me a few pfennigs, when along comes the lady of the house. Why are folks always being given money without doing a scrap of work for it, she says. This man is still pretty fit, why shouldn't he beat the bedroom carpet for it. Well, I lost it. All right, I say, give me your mangy old rug. So your crooked Gustav goes down four flights of stairs, beats the carpet, and back up. Then what does the old bird say? There, my dear chap, now you've earned your five pfennigs . . . And that's a lady!' In the hostel on Gollnowstrasse, the old man now owes for four nights, and unless he can pay for at least two of them, the manager will throw him out.

'How old are you, Grandpa?' 'Seventy-four . . . no, eighty- . . . no, seventy-two.' He's not sure any more. He was born in Posen. He doesn't know if he's German or Polish, and he doesn't really care. When he was a young man, he was the best and most honest milker – he stresses that – on the whole estate. And then the owner threw him out, because a cow had lashed out at him, and he had kicked her in the stomach. But that didn't matter. He had to go into the army anyways. Then there were his years as a hobo. Germany, Austria, Switzerland, Italy, France, and Spain, all on shanks's pony. Years, decades. Till shortly before the Great War, when he found himself back in Germany again as an old man. During the war he worked in some munitions factory, and then a gentleman of the road again. More years.

Till he wound up in Berlin, and the four-million-strong city became his highway because he didn't have enough puff any more. He doesn't know where his parents died, nor where his five brothers and sisters are, if they're even still alive. He has never been inside a cinema. As far as he's concerned, a book is something with stories in it, and the prime function of newspapers is wrapping things up.

But one thing he's learned in his long years of experience, be it in Berlin or Italy or some burg in Silesia: rich people don't do charity. They'd rather turn their dogs loose on beggars or slam doors in their faces. Giving, with a deep reflexive understanding of hunger and misery, is something that only poor people do. The Silesian mineworker, the Italian labourer, the unemployed geezer in Berlin. Tomorrow the old man is headed for proletarian Wedding. He knows and likes the area. 'Coppers, only coppers. But at least they add up,' he says, and pensively puts his hat back on. It feels better to be sitting with his hat on.

In a fit of magnanimity, Fred takes a collection from the gang members, to get together money for the old man's kip. Grand total: two marks, eighty-five pfennigs. The beggar is sceptical when he is given the handful of coppers. They've got to be pulling his leg. But then, when the money's stashed in his pocket, he's in a hurry to leave. Keep what you got. You never know: maybe the boys will drink up their money, and then want it back. It's better to scarper. The manager won't chase him away, he'll get his money . . .

Ludwig keeps noticing more ways in which the gang

has changed. Fred seems to have become treasurer, and each member is called upon to pay a mark a week into the common exchequer. Johnny, Hans, Fred and Konrad have got a regular kip – with Anneliese – at an invalid jailbird's place on Badstrasse. Heinz, Erwin, Walter and Georg seem to have somewhere as well, two of them at a time. Wonder where all this money comes from, thinks Ludwig. He doesn't trust himself to ask.

The boys break up. It's not possible to have a conversation in this crowd. They decide to ride to Schlesischer Bahnhof, and go to Café Messerstich. Why the Messerstich is called a café, and not a bar, is just as obscure as why it's called the Messerstich* in the first place. The clientele is made up of organ-grinders, buskers, ragmen (also known as naturalists), and mainly handicapped male and female beggars. The only thing they like to stab is a piece of roast or at the very least a sausage. The local specialty here are the extraordinary prodigious pigs' feet in jelly. The gang order, and have a slap-up dinner. Gnawed bones are stacked high on the table, the landlord has to send over the road for more rolls. They all eat like combine harvesters.

---

* Messerstich: a stab with a knife. Maybe a jocular debasement of 'Metternich'?

A disabled organ-grinder is propping up the bar. His left sleeve hangs down, loose and empty. His single hand is clutching a large glass of schnapps and raising it to his lips. A sip. The schnapps-wet lips purse themselves in a piercing whistle. As on command, two white rats appear from his two jacket pockets. Clamber nimbly up to his shoulders and perch there on their hind legs, begging. Laughter and applause from the other guests. The disabled rat-tamer feels flattered, takes his half-full glass, and holds it under the noses of both his pets. Each head leans in and sips a tiny amount of the sweet schnapps. Another whistle. The rats scuttle back into their pockets. Contentedly, the man finishes his drink. The animals go with him on his tour. Stand up and beg when they hear the music, disappear up his trouser leg and reappear at his open collar. Ratty Paul is a celebrity in his profession and is reputed to be doing quite well, thanks to his little friends.

The Blood Brothers are sitting replete and idle over their beer. Anneliese is jiggling about on her chair. Casts fearful glances at a table by the stove. A young lad is sitting there, staring aggressively at the Brothers. And if his eyes happen to meet Anneliese's, then she gets even more restless and anxious. Suddenly the boy is standing at the gang's table: 'Can I talk to you, Anneliese.' It sounds brutal and menacing. Anneliese is cravenly on the point of obeying when Jonny leaps up: 'What do you want with her?' 'None of your business, you monkey!' is the ungentle reply. With Jonny's characteristic speed, he lands the fellow an almighty slap. Before the lad knows what's happened to him, he's been hit a second time, and finds himself deposited out on the street. Doesn't dare go back in. 'Who was that, Anneliese?' asks Jonny. Anneliese is crying. 'Oh, you know . . . someone from Friedel Peters's gang.'

Only last week Anneliese was the sweetheart of another gang, namely that of Friedel Peters. But life at Friedel's side no longer suited Anneliese. No one had any money, and one day Friedel had even said to her: 'Anneliese, it's time you went and earned for us.' And so she had gone over to Jonny's mob, because they were flush. Really, Anneliese wasn't behaving any differently than the mistress of some industrialist, who won't hesitate to transfer her affections to a bank executive if heavy industry should fall on hard times and can no longer guarantee her pin money.

'Seems we might get a dust-up later tonight,' says Konrad pensively. 'You could be right,' replies Jonny. 'Franz, ten double Koks!' Fred orders. The prospect of a dust-up requires drink. Jonny owns two knuckle-dusters. He gives one to Konrad, who starts furiously hitting the jagged steel against the table. 'Ten schnapps!' Jonny orders. The drinks in quick succession have the effect of making the boys tense and aggressive. But no one comes to claim Anneliese. Anneliese, who only a moment ago was gibbering with nerves and dread, is now flattered to be the bone of contention between two gangs. For the moment, though, everything in the bar is quiet.

A young man, new to the area, walks into the bar, and enters negotiations with the landlord. An unemployed circus performer of some kind, an acrobat or tumbler. Even though the bar is full to bursting, he gets permission to do some of his stunts. There's an audience for that kind of thing here. A couple of chairs, which the fellow needs as props, are willingly vacated. The guests are aware that something is about to happen, and they mill around the artiste like a great family, full of expectation. A handstand on one hand on the top of the chair-back. The drunken one-armed Ratty Paul grouses from the back: 'Thass nothing, you should see wot I . . .' The artiste does a rubber man, twisting and contorting his body till he is puce in the face. That creates an impression. Everyone is fascinated by the artiste's tricks. Even the landlord is watching now, and the waiter leaves the beers on his tray to go flat.

Now here comes the show-stopper. The artiste picks up one chair between his teeth, and sets the second on top of it. That's the high point of the evening's entertainment. That stunt with the teeth wows them. Not least because they can see the incredible strain in the artiste's face. It's contorted, bright red, the eyes are bulging out of their sockets, his whole body is trembling. The spectators are beside themselves. Ideal moment for the performer to pass the hat around. Result: one mark eighty. Even in penurious circles people pay generously for first-class performance. Ratty Paul buys the artiste a drink. He discreetly wipes the blood off his mouth. His barbarous stunt has left him with bleeding gums.

The performer's feat of strength has done nothing to cool the flickering pugnacity of the Brothers. If only Friedel Peters and his boys would come looking for Anneliese. Boy oh boy, the beer glasses would fly, and the broken chair legs would go whizzing through the air. But there's nothing doing. If they're such cowards that they leave their fellow member's beating unavenged, then too bad. Let's go, we've waited long enough. Where to? How about Auntie Minnie's on Warschauer Brücke. There might be dancing. Jonny pays the bill. Thirty marks. Where do they get the money from, Ludwig thinks again.

The street outside is quiet, no sign of any enemy gang members hanging around. Past Schlesischer Bahnhof, the Blood Brothers turn down on to the deserted Mühlenstrasse. A hundred yards ahead of them, someone scampers across the street, and disappears in the shadow of the house fronts. The gang walks in two lines of four, with the gibbering Anneliese and their youngest, Walter, in the middle of the back. Once again, someone runs across the street. This time they are able to recognise the fellow Jonny slapped around. 'Have you got your knuckleduster, Konrad?' asks Jonny. 'You bet!' Konrad replies. They have walked the hundred yards. Mühlenstrasse widens out into Rummelsburger Platz.

'Go!' comes a shout in the immediate vicinity of the gang. Either side of the Blood Brothers, ten or twelve enemies dart out of dark doorways. The front line of Brothers, with Jonny, and the back line, with Konrad, are prepared. Walter hustles Anneliese to the far side of the road, but he can't stand inaction, and he leaves her in the lurch wailing and jumps right into the knots of tangling boys. Jonny and Konrad's knuckledusters are smashing enemy chins, thumping enemy biceps, slamming down on hard enemy skulls. The fight proceeds in near silence. Both sides know that if there's any noise, a squad car will be there in no time at all, and they'd rather tribal warfare go on without police intervention.

If only there was a bit more light. Blood Brother squares up to Blood Brother, and the same thing is happening with the other mob. Things are already looking critical for the assailants, their skulls are no match for the knuckledusters. Then a shot rings out. Bang! Like a whiplash. Walter wobbles into the gutter, clasping his left arm. 'Oo . . . oo . . . ow!' The shot, the cry of the wounded boy, are signs that the Peters gang has had enough. They flee. The Blood Brothers have won the day, and they stand there panting and tending to Walter, who is still screaming his 'Ooo . . . oow!' into the silence.

Windows are already being thrown open. Bed jackets and string vests shiver and shout 'Murder!' and 'Police!' and 'Help!' 'Let's go!' orders Jonny. They run off in the direction of Schlesischer Bahnhof. Jonny and Konrad support Walter. Ludwig and Georg have taken charge of the whimpering Anneliese. On Fruchtstrasse, Jonny and Konrad manage to stop a cab, push Walter inside, and jump in after him. Jonny calls out of the window: 'Come after . . . Badstrasse!' And then the scene is over. The gang breaks up into twos. They take a fleet of taxis to Badstrasse.

Gotthelf, ex-jailbird, now responsible gang-godfather, is not especially surprised when his charges turn up with the injured Walter. 'That's Berlin for you,' he says, and examines the wounded boy. Luckily, it's just a flesh wound. Konrad arrives with some bandages bought from a twenty-four-hour pharmacy. In dribs and drabs the other Brothers arrive. Walter's wound is washed and bandaged up. Should he see a doctor tomorrow? A risk. The doctor will ask questions. But Gotthelf has a solution. There's this tame apothecary he knows, who's taken to drink. He'll treat Walter. Walter is feeling rather perky. He likes this role, he likes the attention, and his wound isn't especially painful. He needs to get some sleep. First he knocks back a hefty schnapps. 'Schnapps is always good!' proclaims the wise Gotthelf.

It's three in the morning. Konrad and Jonny, Hans and Fred are at home. Jonny will share Hans's bed, so that Walter gets an uninterrupted night. Those boys who aren't staying at Gotthelf's take their leave. Anneliese is with Ludwig for tonight, and she walks back with him to his new pad on Grenadierstrasse.

THIRTEEN

After two nights, the modest lucky streak of overnight snow is over. Rain, endless and monotonous, dribbles on to the asphalt. Rain that softens up ancient shoes, till the unhappy wearer has the impression of going around in sodden dishcloths.

Willi Kludas is standing out on Neukölln's Hermannplatz at night, staring vacantly at the illuminating and then disappearing advertisement of a brown bear* the size of a house lighting a cigarette

---

* The bear is the emblem of Berlin and the origin of the city's name.

and complacently blowing out a stream of light-bulb smoke, with the legend: *Berlin smokes Juno.*

There was no more staying at Silesian Olga's. She had given him a couple of nights' credit. After that she wanted to be paid, either in money or her usual tribute. And that wasn't on, not least with his condition. Oh, the condition. On top of everything else. The first girl he'd ever slept with. The evening after, he had hung around looking for Elly and given her the address in Köllnischer Park. I'll be back here tomorrow. If you're not able to show me a card like mine, then I'll report you to the police, he had threatened her curtly, and then he had gone. The next evening Elly was waiting for him, with her grey card. He had inspected the card, and ignored Elly. Nothing to eat, nowhere to stay and a disgusting disease. Shit! He had to lug his medicine around with him wherever he went. Where could he have left it anyway? You'll be over it in three or four days, the doc had said. And the blood test had come up all right. Negative, was the message for him at the end of three days.

If only the bloody rain would stop. Forever standing in doorways. Till a policeman asks him what he's doing. The big bars over the road, how full they are. The people inside them are all right. They're smoking their Junos, and eating and drinking, and relaxing in the warm. What if he went into the Bräustübl, and just

132

stood by a table? It's so packed, surely no one would notice that he wasn't ordering anything. At least get his rags dry, and stand in the warm for a bit.

He crosses the street and walks into the bar. Pushes his way through the customers, and goes through to the toilets at the back. Then he will slowly make his way to his place by the table next to the stove. There's enough empty glasses standing around as well, he's just finished his drink and is waiting to see whether he'll order another. That's right, isn't it? . . . In the toilet, Willi makes a few adjustments to his appearance. Squeezes the wet out of his trouser legs and his jacket. My God, the water . . . He takes a drink from the cold tap. I'm just having my beer in the bog, he thinks. Smartly, as if he had silver money, he makes his way out through the bar. No one pays him any mind as he draws up at his place. In front of him is a half-full glass of beer. Is the owner gone? Wait and see.

He presses his bum against the heater. Jesus, that feels good. But before long he needs to move again, the wet fabric is steaming as if it was just out of the washing cauldron. The people standing round the table with him are starting to pass remarks. Go on, laugh, you mugs. You can smoke and drink, and if you were hungry, you could probably get yourselves a sausage from the bar. And I expect you're fixed up for the night. No one shows up to drink the half-glass in front of Willi. Probably left, had so much he can't take any more. Willi takes a gander at the clock over the bar: almost two o'clock. At seven he can go to the warming hall. Five hours. The table clears. At long last, Willi claims the flat beer for himself. Now he's good till three o'clock without anyone throwing him out.

A new client, a young fellow like Willi, walks up to the bar. Gets a glass of beer from the barman along with twenty-five cigarettes, and walks up to Willi's table. He's not short, thinks Willi, a pack of twenty-five. The stranger sips at his beer, lights a cigarette, and looks up quickly at Willi. They stare at each other. Damn, that face is familiar, they both think at the same time. Willi thinks he knows the boy. A couple of minutes pass. Each of them is turning over his memories for the answer to the tormenting question: Where do I know him from? The boys are circling each other, but neither dares to ask the other.

Till the stranger takes the plunge and addresses Willi directly: 'Don't I know you from somewhere?' 'I've got that feeling too . . .' replies Willi. 'Weren't you in welfare in H.?' the stranger goes on to ask. Then the penny drops for Willi: 'Ludwig! Christ Almighty, what are you doing here?' And Ludwig is in the picture as well: 'You're Willi, aincha? Willi from Dorm Two, isn't that right?' 'You bet!' Two old boys from H. have found each other. Ludwig ran away two years ago, Willi only two weeks. 'What are the odds on that!' 'Wow, Ludwig, amazing.' 'Shall we sit down somewhere?' Ludwig proposes. 'I'm skint,' replies Willi. 'Never mind that, Willi, it's fine, I've got money.'

They find a little table for themselves. Ludwig has learned not to make a distinction between being skint and being famished. So he asks right away: 'What are you having to eat, Willi?' and thrusts the menu over to him. 'Maybe a sausage or something . . .' 'Maybe you'll have something else! You want something proper and hot.' He takes a look at the menu himself. 'Pigs' feet, and a bowl of pea soup for starters,' he decides, on Willi's behalf. Ludwig orders Willi's meal, and a pint and a short for both of them. Joy at the reunion shows in their eyes. The joy of having found a comrade, a veteran from the same institution. The joy of telling one version and hearing another of how they managed to run away. 'Here, you eat first,' says Ludwig, and he starts on his account of his escape from H. And when Ludwig asks: 'Do you remember how little Heini and me . . .' and 'Can you remember how the director . . .' then Willi, cheeks bulging, can only answer urgently and in full agreement, with 'Hmm . . .' and 'Hmm . . .'

So Ludwig tells his story. Of his wanderings till he got to Berlin, where he'd never been before. Of the hunger, the nights on freight trains, in condemned buildings and on waste ground. Of selling his body to keep from starving like a miserable alley cat. Of occasional acts of theft. Till he fell in with the Blood Brothers. And then the experiences of the last few months: prison, how he got away from the escort. 'So now I'm legit, and I go by August Kaiweit,' concludes Ludwig. Willi tells his adventures of the past few weeks. Many details are common with the experiences of Ludwig, and hundreds of other boys who prefer starving at liberty to being half-fed in welfare. Ludwig has decided that Willi is to join the gang. He'll fix it with Jonny so that Willi is spared the apprenticeship rituals. And Willi is going to take the chance with both hands. He dreads being on his own again, in the heartless endless wastes of Berlin. If you've got mates, everything is much easier. Last orders are called. Arm in arm, the two boys wander off to the night bus. For the time being, Willi is staying at Ludwig's.

The following morning Willi is introduced to the gang in the Rückerklause. Everyone's there. Even Walter. He's got his left arm in a sling, and is quite the hero. Jonny looks Willi over and gives him the third degree. A stranger, someone he doesn't know from Adam, so everything he says could be a lie, being adopted into the gang? No way. But that's not quite

136

the situation here. He's got Ludwig vouching for him. Jonny doesn't mind adding a new member. It's up to the boys to say what they want. If Ludwig is of the opinion that Willi'd be an asset, that's fine by him. Willi is welcomed to the gang with a shaking of hands all round. A solemn drink will give the new member-ship legal force.

'Gang baptism?' the hero Walter asks slyly. Willi might be excused the apprenticeship that would have had him polishing everyone else's shoes, but no one gets out of gang baptism. That's obligatory. And if he fails at the baptism, which is at the same time the journeyman's piece, then he'll retake it until he passes. Without a successful baptism, no one is worthy of full membership of the Brothers. Baptism with the Brothers takes the form of completing the act of sexual intercourse four times in the space of an hour, with the whole gang watching, and invited guests as well. In view of Willi's condition, the baptism is postponed till the doctor gives him the all-clear.

Evening. The gang are sitting in Max's in Linienstrasse. Ludwig and Willi are expected any minute. Jonny splits everyone up into three groups, and gives them their mission: a supermarket in the east. Tomorrow is the last of the month, and the shops will be doing booming business. Best moment for pickpocketing. The head of each band of three will lift the purse and give it right away to the second man, who'll slip it to the third. The three groups will work independently of each other in the shop. The gang has been doing this for months now. In department stores and weekly markets and market halls.

Generally, it's the thin change-purses of working-class mothers that get it. You just need to reach into the shopping baskets, the nets and the pockets. The money's lying on top. The support, the weekly wage, a whole month's pay. It was Fred who set the gang on the path of pickpocketing. The idea turned out to be so brilliant that they've been flush ever since. As long as Ludwig was in prison, everything went well. The day Ludwig turned up, Jonny gave orders not to tell Ludwig anything about the source of the gang's money for now. Jonny had a notion that Ludwig wouldn't be a willing participant in these escapades. He thought he might have to do something to talk him round first. Ply him with money and then, if Ludwig showed distaste or alarm, to confront him with it: What are you on about? You were happy to take our money, weren't you? You didn't think we'd won the lottery? So don't be a mug, and roll your sleeves up.

Willi walks into the bar in a high state of excitement, no Ludwig: 'You're all to go to Schmidt's. Ludwig's waiting there. He's got the piece of work who gave him the ticket!' Damn it! The excitement. To Schmidt's, right away. In separate groups, unobtrusively as ever. Ludwig is sitting at a table near the band. Jonny, Willi and Fred join him, the others hang around near the door. In case the fellow tries to do a runner . . . That's him at the back, with his girl. A geezer of twenty-odd, sharp suit, nice coat, well turned out. 'Are you quite sure it's him, Ludwig?' asks Jonny. 'Positive!' Jonny walks up to the table. In his curt decisive way, he asks the little spiv to follow him out back.

In a corner, Jonny indicates Ludwig, who is there as well. 'Here, I expect you remember my friend?' 'What's all this about? I've never seen you before, either of you,' replies the stranger. Now Ludwig remembers the voice as well. 'Let me remind you then . . . Stettiner Bahnhof . . . The left-luggage ticket . . .' Ludwig says slowly. The spiv flushes red and turns pale, then he tries to brazen it out: 'Oh, you're that swindler! You stole the suitcase and stiffed me!' Jonny's fist makes short hard contact with the point of his chin. 'Listen, fellow. My friend here has done eight weeks in remand for you, and was sentenced to four months. You can choose what you want to do: either we'll find a copper and get you sent down, or else you come along with us like a good fellow. This thing needs sorting out, wouldn't you say?'

139

The spiv stands, pale and shaking, by the wall. 'Go with you where?' 'Leave that up to us. We're not going to kill you. Tell your sweetheart you've been called away, and come with us.' The fellow goes over to the girl, Jonny and Fred are waiting at the door. 'Where are we taking him, Jonny?' 'To Ulli's summer house, Koloniestrasse.' Fred goes ahead in a taxi, to alert Ulli. The spiv walks out, flanked by Jonny and Ludwig. The other Blood Brothers follow at a suitable distance.

By the time they get to the summer house, everything has been prepared for bringing the miscreant to justice. Ulli, the chief, is present with a few of his boys. A sentry is posted to guard against surprises. Ulli, who doesn't have a dog in this fight, acts as the impartial judge. Jonny is the prosecutor, Ludwig the star witness. The accused is seated on the same orange crate that a while ago served as a drinks cabinet on the occasion of Ulli's birthday. Heinz is instructed to defend. The accused says his name is Hermann Plettner. What did he live on, asks Judge Ulli. 'None of your beeswax!' 'Ever been in welfare?' 'Oh, leave it out!' Then Ludwig describes what happened. How Hermann approached him outside Aschinger's, gave him the ticket and a mark, and how he, Ludwig, was subsequently arrested. Now it's the turn of the defendant. 'I never knew that chit was hot. I picked it up off the pavement.'

Prosecutor Jonny speaks: 'A particularly low-grade

villain . . . he should have admitted he'd stolen the ticket and gone shares with Ludwig. That would have been on the level. But this here is a crook who's too much of a coward to get the chestnuts out of the fire himself, and would rather involve an innocent party, for a mealy mark, claiming the chit was his property. Such a person is a villain who deserves no sympathy. Fit punishment, in my view, is twenty-five blows with a dog whip on his bare behind. Should the accused refuse the punishment, then have him handed over to the police without further ado . . .'

Hermann Plettner leaped to his feet when he heard the punishment. His defendant Heinz can only point to the outside possibility that the ticket had actually been found and picked up by the defendant. 'Whether he stole it or found it, it's moot. All we need to know is that the bastard lied, in the full knowledge that Ludwig would have to pay with his freedom,' Jonny intervened.

Judge Ulli withdraws to consider his verdict. By the time he returns to the summer house, the accused is already in tears. Verdict: handed over to the police or twenty-five lashes with the dog whip. After each set of ten strokes, an interval of ten minutes. Punishment to be with immediate effect. Hermann Plettner is lying curled up in the corner in a ball, whimpering. 'So what's it to be then? Police or whipping?' Jonny asks, unmoved. The condemned man slithers across to Jonny on his knees, says to Ludwig: 'Please, please, let me go . . . I'll give you . . . here, my watch, my money . . . there's over twenty marks there . . . let me go!' 'Police or whipping? Make up your mind, will you?' Howling, begging, wailing, but no answer. 'All right then, police. Ludwig, come with us,' decrees Jonny. 'No, no . . . beat me.' So it's the whipping.

The orange crate is moved to the centre of the room. Who's the executioner? Ludwig, you? Ludwig quickly declines. Fred volunteers for the task, strips off coat and jacket, and stands there with the leather dog whip in his hand. 'Trousers off, Plettner!' The condemned man has to lie across the crate. Two boys hold his legs, two more press his face into his balled-up trousers, to stifle his cries of pain. The first blow comes hissing down on the naked flesh. The body rears up, and the four assistants need all their strength to hold on. There's a soft gurgling crying through the trousers. Blow after blow comes down. Jonny counts them coldly and pitilessly. Ludwig turns away. The first set of ten lashes.

A ten minute break. Plettner is lying next to the crate. The welts across his arse are swelling, blood-red. 'Please, please . . . no more . . .' the whimpering begins again. 'Enough,' says Jonny. The next lashes slice open the swollen skin across the welts. Blood

142

spurts out, starts to trickle down the thighs. Implacable, not letting up in the least, Fred completes the second set of ten. Plettner's bottom is a bloody mess. Plettner is draped motionless across the crate. 'Water,' says Jonny. Half a bucket is emptied over Plettner's head and the blood is washed off. 'Jonny, that's enough,' says Ludwig. It's Ulli's decision whether Plettner is to receive the remaining five lashes or not. 'All right, let him go.'

It's not so easy. Stood up on his feet, Plettner promptly crumples in a heap. Someone is told to go for schnapps. Wet handkerchiefs are placed on the raw bleeding buttocks, and then the punished criminal gets his trousers put back on. He is lying on his front, wailing quietly like a little child. A shot of rum brings him round. Jonny addresses him: 'You've been spared the last five lashes. You can thank Ludwig for that. As far as we're concerned, the business is at an end. If you're sensible, it's over for you too. You know we can find you any time.'

'Shouldn't he thank us for the lashes?' butts in Fred, apparently still not satisfied. 'Yes, he should say thank you, that's only right,' Ulli concurs. Hermann Plettner is forced to thank his punishers. He hobbles over to Ulli: 'Er . . . thank you.' 'No, no, boy, that won't do. You have to say: thank you very much for my lashes.' Plettner begins again: '. . . thank you . . .

143

very much . . . for . . . my . . . lashes.' Then Fred trumps everyone. He forces Plettner to kiss the whip that has his blood on it. Two boys escort him out to Koloniestrasse. They watch him unsteadily feel his way along the plank fencing . . . The gang's court of justice has bloodily avenged the despicable deed.

FOURTEEN

Jonny is having a private meeting with Ludwig and Willi. 'This afternoon we're going on the job. First, I just want you to watch how it's done. I want you, Ludwig, to be attached to Fred's group, and you, Willi, come along with me. I just want you to watch today, to observe and learn.' Now, at last, Ludwig knows where the money comes from. Pickpocketing! Ludwig has no chance to talk it over with Willi. Both of them listen in silence to Jonny's revelations. For today, they are there in a purely passive role. They won't agree to be involved in any actual stealing. That's what both of them decide for themselves, and they resolve to talk about it with each other at the next opportunity.

The gang splits up at Alexanderplatz. Each group makes their own way east. Ludwig follows Fred, Willi walks along after Jonny. Fred's band are detailed to work on the ground floor of the department store, Jonny's section in the food hall, and Konrad and Hans are to work the elevators. Ludwig sees Fred press himself against a sale counter, which is thronged with housewives. The other two push in behind him, Fred is pressed against the women. These few seconds Fred takes advantage of. His hand slips into a canvas shopping bag. A little purse is swiftly transferred from Fred to Georg, and from Georg to Erwin. Fred moves off. So do Georg and Erwin.

The elevator gives a little jerk that sends Konrad barging into a woman. He begs pardon. Behind his back, his hand passes on a little purse . . .

Jonny heads for a stand where deep-frozen geese are on sale. An incredible pushing and shoving, because of the cheap wares. The eyes of the customers are all on the geese, and with one hand they test the goods. Jammed in between them are their shopping nets and bags. It's like stealing candy, thinks Jonny, passing a purse on. After each strike the band is under instructions to go to a different part of the store. No more than one hour in the building as a whole. Then each group makes its own way back to headquarters on Badstrasse.

The gang are sitting in the windowless back room, sorting through the pickings. Five change purses and three little wallets, which are immediately fed to the flames. One wallet has the jackpot: four fifty-mark notes, the other two contain a total of ninety marks. The five purses contain one hundred and eight marks, forty pfennigs in all. Stamps, receipts and other papers are also burned. The takings of one single hour: three hundred and ninety-eight marks, forty pfennigs! Ludwig and Willi sit there in amazement. They try desperately to convey delight as the others do. But their eyes express chiefly fear and shock. 'Well, what do you say to that, Ludwig and Willi? Nice line of business?' asks Fred. 'If it wasn't for me, all of youse would still be broke!' he crows. Gotthelf gets his share: twenty marks. Each of the boys gets thirty marks. What's left goes into Fred's keeping, he's the treasurer. Ludwig and Willi pocket their share. If they refused it, that would be tantamount to betrayal, and they would be looking at arse tartare like Plettner's.

They arrange to meet up at ten in the *Auto-topp*. Anneliese will be there too, so it'll be a jolly evening. Till then, they're all left to their own devices. Money's not a problem, anyway.

Ludwig and Willi sit down in a bar and ponder.

What are they going to do? Trying to talk the gang out of thieving is senseless. Every gang is either 'for us or against us'. For us? 'No, Ludwig, I'm not doing that!' 'No, me neither, Willi.' Against us, then? That's no better. 'You can do what you like. But we want no part of it, isn't that right, Willi?' 'Yes, Ludwig, but we can't tell them that.' 'Then we leave the gang.' Alone again. All alone again in Berlin? Willi remembers the terrible nights and days of homelessness and hunger. But he's got Ludwig now. If there's two, it's not quite so bad. 'What about the thirty marks? Do we give them back, or hang on to them?' asks Ludwig. He supplies the answer himself: 'If we give them back, we'd be starting off broke.' 'I think it's better we keep them . . .' says Willi, slowly and quietly, 'I mean, it's not as though the housewives are going to get them back or anything.'

They decide to disappear. The gang's first thought will be that they've been arrested. The police are looking for both of them. Of course, it means giving up the Grenadierstrasse digs; that would be the first place the gang looked. It means giving up the odds and ends of property they've got in there; if they went back for anything, then Jonny would know the score. 'We need to leave the Münzstrasse area, Willi. We're too well known there.' 'So where do we go?' Their decision doesn't exactly make them happy, too many times already they've known what it is not to have a penny in their pockets. But to go on the job with the gang? They might as well hand themselves into the police right away. It's inevitable that the gang will one day get caught. 'And you, Willi, you're twenty-one soon, so you're done with child welfare. Then you can go around everywhere and say: my name's Willi Kludas, and I want papers and I want unemployment . . . Your position is different from mine. I'm nineteen. They can keep me for another two years. But I'd rather go stealing from the rich if I'm skint. What the gang's doing . . . they're stealing from people that haven't got much themselves. Did you see, there was an unemployment card in one of the purses. Those people will be hungry . . .'

They sit over their beer, pondering. No valid papers, wanted by the police, and go straight? That's a trick no one's yet pulled off, Ludwig and Willi. Only bettered by having no documents at all and trying to lead a law-abiding life! Go back to the institution you've run away from. Show some remorse and accept what's coming. Take your reprimands and the occasional slap until you're twenty-one. Then they may deal with you generously . . .

Ludwig and Willi trudge through the crowds and lights of Tauentzienstrasse. They feel they are in a foreign city. What's Berlin? As far as they were concerned,

Berlin was Münzstrasse and Schlesischer Bahnhof. It never occurred to them to go to the west of the city. Grey streets with one yard and then another behind and then maybe a third, that was home to them. Here they feel they're somewhere else. In a rich and cheerful abroad, as it would appear. Everyone is wearing brand-new clothes, as though it were a holiday and not some ordinary Wednesday. The shops are like palaces, in which His Majesty the customer* is standing around idly, on the lookout for some precious knick-knack or other. And the women – the ladies. Every one, apparently without exception, well dressed, fragrant, lovely. Even the little dogs the ladies press to their furs, or have trotting along beside them, are dressed in cute little blankets and have sparkling collars. And a dog, one little dog, a tiny bundle of fluff, actually wears little patent leather booties on all four feet. 'Did you catch that, Willi?'

A rich and beautiful abroad. What are two beggars doing here? They don't belong in the area. They've come from the other Berlin, from some musty cellar or squalid back building, to beg here. The other Berlin . . . There won't be any hostels here like Silesian Olga's. And there are almost no boys like themselves.

———

* A German phrase that says the customer is king; used in a purely ironic sense during the GDR's existence.

If there are, then they're on the hustle. Some are completely newly clad, if you walk along behind them, you can see that they've never even had their boots resoled, you can see the fresh leather gleaming under the arch between heel and sole. Their trousers are fashionably baggy and have a sharp crease. And the boys' smell . . . oh, pomade, scent, aftershave. They must be raking it in.

Such are the thoughts of Willi and Ludwig as they move around the other, the western Berlin. They have decided to steer clear of their home turf around the Alex and Schlesischer Bahnhof for the time being, so as not to run into the Blood Brothers. Willi hasn't been out west for four years. And this is the first time Ludwig has ever clapped eyes on Tauentzienstrasse. Once or twice he'd been as far as the Bülowbogen. Now they're standing on the corner of Kurfürstendamm and Joachimstaler Strasse, gawping at the wonders, allowing the endless columns of cars to pass, watching the light-shows of the madly appealing advertisements, allowing themselves to be barged and pushed out of the way. In a beer hall opposite Bahnhof Zoo, they eat a sausage and have a glass of beer. Then they stroll on. Without any aim in mind, following their noses, till they're suddenly back at Bahnhof Zoo again. They stop under the meeting-point clock. 'What'll we do, Ludwig? It's almost midnight.'

151

Two elderly gentlemen in furs are watching Willi and Ludwig, then they consult each other, and walk up to the boys. 'Good evening, lads.' Willi and Ludwig jump. Police? Nah, won't be, not smelling of scent like that. 'Not hooked up with anyone yet, you two cuties?' Willi and Ludwig look at each other: they must think we're tarts. 'Come and have a drink?' asks the persistent gentleman. 'Where?' says Ludwig finally, asking a question of his own. 'Oh my goodness, somewhere nice . . .' 'What about the Silhouette?' suggests his companion. 'We don't know that place,' Willi says. 'What about letting us take you there?' 'All right, and we'll have a drink, won't we, Willi?' 'Orright.'

To Geisbergstrasse. The two lads are pushed through a doorway. When they part the curtains inside the door, they recoil and turn to leave. 'What's the matter, boys?' Ludwig mumbles something about working clothes and being badly dressed . . . such an elegant place . . . 'Pah, nonsense!' Then they're in the restaurant, and are welcomed by a man in a tuxedo. 'The cloakroom is this way.' The two gentlemen take off their furs, and are standing in tuxedos too. Ludwig allows the maître d' to take his coat, and stands there in his tattered jacket and defunct tracksuit bottoms. Willi doesn't have a coat to part with. Someone else has got his anorak, and his suit hasn't been the same since the Cologne–Berlin express. Willi blushes pink, and holds his hand in front of his bare throat. But neither the gentlemen nor the maître d', nor the other no-less-elegant guests, are at all put out by the boys' style. On the contrary, plenty of admiring looks go Ludwig and Willi's way.

The two tuxes link arms with the boys, and conduct them into a little booth. While the gentlemen are busy choosing drinks, the boys take stock of their surroundings. The Silhouette is small, intimate, and the theme of the decor is a flaring provocative red. At the front, a bar and tables; left and right, little private booths. The wall coverings are red, as are the soft carpets; the lampshades are a glowing red. A sultry atmosphere, languorously underscored by the music. Gentlemen in stylish evening dress or tuxedos; ladies in full-length gowns with bare arms and half-bared bosoms. An overheated atmosphere of intense warped eroticism: women trying to catch the eyes of girls, men aroused by male flesh. No loud speech, no full-throated laughter. It's hanging in the air like an explosive.

With their forthright and uncouth boyishness, Willi and Ludwig have aroused a certain amount of interest. Desires, weary of bathed and anointed bodies, flicker to life at the sight of the less clean, but rawer, prospect of these working-class boys. The waiter, polished as he is, brings sharply aromatic brandies in iridescent bumpers. He brings cigarettes. Ten pfennigs, the boys read on the stamp. The brandy flows down their throats like burning oil. Another, then a third, bring disinhibition. Willi and Ludwig fall into the '*Du*' form with the two tuxes, and relate escapades from their time in various homes.

A few hours ago, Ludwig and Willi watched the smart boy-prostitutes on Tauentzienstrasse and thought: they're going with gentlemen into nice hotels to climb between white sheets . . . At three in the morning, two taxis draw up in front of a private hotel off the Kurfürstendamm. The two tuxes and the two boys, drunk and apathetic, walk in. Ludwig and Willi's first night in the west of Berlin. The way from the north and east of the city to the west often seems to lead through the sheets of a private hotel.

FIFTEEN

At noon, Willi and Ludwig are woken by the sound of a plangent voice at the door. The chubby descant of a woman outside calls upon the two gutter-snipes to vacate the premises. Gradually it dawns on the boys where they are. In the white sheets of a private hotel. The distinguished gentlemen left after a while, and had each deposited a twenty-mark note. The distinguished gentlemen! Along with their silk-lined tuxes they had stripped off their manners. What was left were two scrawny little men whose wallets allowed them to buy young healthy, if half-starved, boys. Details of the night just past swim into the boys' consciousness. 'Yuck!' says Ludwig. 'Yes, it makes me feel sick. Never again . . .'

They get dressed. The madam walks into the room without looking at the boys. She checks the beds, the wardrobe, goes through the whole inventory of the ruddy room. 'Too bad you had to come along, we were just about to steal the fitted wardrobe,' Ludwig says cheekily.

They eat lunch at Aschinger's. They've each got over fifty marks. 'You know, Ludwig,' Willi begins, 'I can't stand it here. Where are we going to sleep? Hadn't we better go back up north?' 'But where? The gang's got tentacles everywhere!' 'What about Neukölln?' suggests Willi. 'Neukölln? Jonny doesn't get down there much. Sure, let's go there. We can't handle Kurfürstendamm.'

In the café of the department store on Hermannplatz, they brainstorm. What can we do with our money, the hundred marks? What line of work should we invest it in? Because one thing's for sure, we're going to have to work, yes, and we want to as well. Anything not to have to go back to the Brothers and rob working wives' purses. Shall we deal? In razorblades, or bananas, or newspapers, or patented stain-removers? Sell neckties for thirty-five pfennigs at the weekly markets, or lace or stockings? Eh, eh? But each time they hit an insuperable obstacle: no papers! Any

156

policeman can take them in for trading without a licence. 'No, Ludwig, all that's not on.' 'But what do we do then, once we've got through our cash? What, Willi?' 'Then our shitty old life begins again . . .' He sounds like a man about to commit suicide, the gas turned on, about to say his last words. 'How great it would be, Willi, if we didn't have to worry about welfare . . . if we had some proper papers . . .'

For a moment, neither of them speaks. All around them, the noise of the overfilled refreshment room. Busy people sitting over a drink. With the rim of the cup against their lip, they suddenly remember: Oh yes, I wanted pressure buttons. Or: August wanted to try some of those jellied prawns! The cup clinks down on its saucer, and the person rushes over to the elevator. But there are also people here with too much time on their hands. Time is the only thing they have. There are no anxious waiters hovering here; here, when home is a cold and unlit hole, you can sit for six or eight hours over a cheap coffee.

'Hey, Willi,' Ludwig breaks the silence a little unwillingly, 'you know something we could try? I've talked to some guys who've done it, and done all right with it.' 'Well, what, what is it?' 'Listen, Willi. We take a sack. A sack each – one for you, one for me. Then we go from house to house and we say: Hello, good morning, we pay top whack for old boots and shoes, as much as two marks a pair. Do you have any to sell? And then, when they show us their stuff, we make a face, and keep making a face, and in the end we just pay ten or twenty pfennigs apiece. When our sacks are full, we take all the shoes and boots, and polish them and shine them up. We could even get some cheap pieces of leather, and straighten a heel, or put a patch on a sole. Then when every-thing's hunky-dory, we sell the whole lot to junk dealers!' Ludwig stops and looks expectantly into Willi's face. 'Well, go on, what do you think?' 'Do you think we'll manage to flog that old junk?' 'Flog it?' crows Ludwig, 'Do you think some unemployed geezer can afford top of the line shoes at Salamander? Our old junk will be the best stuff going!' 'But where will we get hold of a place to kip and work on these shoes?' asks Willi. 'Yeah, I know, a place. Without papers. I've got papers in the name of Kaiweit of course, but I can't let the police see those . . .' says Ludwig.

For the past six months, the pensioner Frieda Bauerbach has had a sign out: *Room to let to 1 or 2 gentlemen. See Bauerbach. Yard, 1. Cellar, left.* 'Shall we give it a go, Willi?' 'No harm in trying.' No sunbeam has ever succeeded in illuminating the depths of widow Bauerbach's basement bedsit, and daylight can only be induced to produce a blue shimmer in the cellar by means of an ingenious arrangement of mirrors. A friendly lady of sixty-odd opens to their knocking. Come about the room? 'Yes, for me and my brother,' replies Ludwig.

The back room is spacious and has a large window. What it looks on to: a sprawling heap of junk. Inventory of the room: two iron bedsteads, a table, a wardrobe, three chairs and a washstand. In the darkest corner lurks a hideous plush sofa. Rent, for two occupants: ten marks per week, including coffee, excluding rolls, heat and gas. The 'brothers' Ludwig and Willi eye one another questioningly. 'We'll take it,' says Ludwig. 'Our name's Kaiweit. He's Willi and I'm Ludwig. We'll register with the police tomorrow. And now listen, madam. We're in business. We buy old shoes and resell them. And we mean to bring all the shoes we buy, a sack of them a day, back here and clean them up. Is that all right with you?' Frau Bauerbach is agreed. She offers up a still darker kitchen space. The shoes could be cleaned and stored there. 'Business is business. Main thing is, it's an honest business,' says Frau Bauerbach with preacherly dignity. 'Here's the first week's rent in advance, and we'll bring in our things later.' They are given a set of keys, and Frau Bauerbach goes out with a chair, to at last take down her sign.

'Now let's get going, Willi!' They make for the

shops. First sacks; they're only thirty pfennigs. Then big pots of shoe-polish, and an array of brushes and laces. A few pounds of scrap leather, an iron tripod, various nails and hammers and pliers, things a cobbler might need. For their own needs, some cheap linen, toiletries, and some food items so that they only need to eat out once a day. Everything is stowed in two large cardboard boxes. Then they go back home. Home . . . how that sounds . . . Home is Ziethenstrasse in Neukölln.

In the meantime, Frau Bauerbach has made their room a little more comfortable. The sofa's arms and back are resplendent under white crocheted throws, there are patchwork rugs next to their beds, and everywhere freshly dusted baubles catch the eye. Frau Bauerbach has even gone to the trouble of getting a new mantle for the gaslight. And if the gentlemen – 'Hear that, Willi, gentlemen!?' – have any wishes, a cup of coffee or tea, then Frau Bauerbach will be only too glad to oblige. Happy, with flaming cheeks, the boys stand in their room: yes, indeed, their room! Not in a welfare dorm, not in a hostel, no: furnished gentlemen, in their own room! They unpack their purchases, carry the tools and the leather into the little cubbyhole that will be their workshop. Here, too, Frau Bauerbach has donated a mantle to the rusty old gaslight. Willi goes out for wood and coke briquettes, and before long the Dutch oven is radiating heat.

The lamp is lit, the table pushed up to the sofa, and Frau Bauerbach brings them coffee for their supper, as requested. In a mighty brown pot, there it is, steaming on the table. Frau Bauerbach has supplied them with cups and cutlery too. And here comes the solemn moment when Willi and Ludwig settle down on the sofa to begin supper. Not a dry roll and beer, like in the bar. No, a real homely supper. They look at each other but don't speak. The moment is too much. They have their own place, after all that dirt, after so much doing without . . . After supper they each settle into their corner of the sofa, smoking and thinking about tomorrow's tour. Their debut as boot-buyers. Frau Bauerbach comes in one last time, and brings an alarm clock. They set it for eight o'clock, and then they go to sleep.

At nine the next morning, they pick up their rolled-up sacks, jam them under their arms, and get small change for ten marks from the post office. As a man of business, you always have to have the correct change, the clientele wants to be paid quickly and promptly. Streets left of Berliner Strasse have been set as the field of operations. On the way there, they practise their line: 'Good morning. We're paying up to two marks for old shoes – have you got any you're looking to sell?'

Isn't this a good omen? From the first – the very first – woman they acquire two pairs of gents' shoes, brown and black. After a bit of back and forth, Ludwig shells out sixty pfennigs. Into the sack they go. Here the door isn't even opened, they see the suspicious eyes at the peephole. In another place, the whole family is employed to scout around corners and look out for old shoes. Payment is in cash, and cash money in proletarian Neukölln is a rare commodity. At the end of two hours they have paid out two marks eighty and have acquired nine pairs of shoes. They go remorselessly up stairs and down: 'Good morning, We're paying . . .' We're paying, those are the magic words. By two o'clock both their sacks are full. The boys have lost count of how many pairs. They've paid out around eight marks.

Home, to Mother Bauerbach's. Dump the sacks in the workshop, quickly grab some lunch, and then get to sorting and repairing and cleaning. They gulp down their fifty pfennigs' worth of lunch, smoke a cigarette on the way home. They tie on aprons made of old sacking, and then it's to the workshop. The shoes tumble out of the sacks on to the floor. Each pair was laced together upon acquisition. First, those pairs needing repair are sorted out. Ludwig gets out nails and tools, and sets to work. A patch on a heel here, another on a toecap there. Willi gets to brushing and polishing. They work without looking up, hardly talking. Every so often, a puff at a cigarette. By eight at night, twenty-two pairs of shoes and seven pairs of boots are standing in a row. Clean, shining, fixed up. Ludwig and Willi inspect their troops, and each pair is given a number that is entered on a list, together with the price it is expected to bring from the junk man. According to the list, the total for twenty-nine pairs will be twenty-one marks and forty pfennigs. A clear profit of thirteen marks. 'Well, let's see if we get that much,' says Willi laconically. For tomorrow, only three hours of acquisitions are planned. In the afternoon, they need to dispose of the twenty-nine pairs. To dealers on Linienstrasse, Grosse Hamburger Strasse, Ackerstrasse and Auguststrasse. They will have to keep their eyes peeled for any Brothers. After supper, they crawl into bed, exhausted.

Linienstrasse, the section between Neue König- and Prenzlauer Strasse, is all second-hand dealers, one after another. They all deal in old shoes. Ludwig stumbles down into one basement. Willi waits on the street with the sacks. 'Come on down!' calls Ludwig. The sacks are emptied out in front of the counter, and the dealer picks out what he thinks he can use. Eleven pairs meet his standards. Price? Ludwig notes the numbers, consults his list: 'Those eleven pairs . . . come to . . . eight marks twenty.' The dealer checks

each individual shoe and boot, frowns, as the boys
had done when they were buying. He offers them
seven marks. Ludwig wants seven-fifty, and they
finally settle on seven marks and twenty-five pfennigs.
Their first transaction is in the bag. They undertake
to supply the dealer on a regular basis. Outside,
Ludwig is jubilant: 'That's a great price! Thirty pfennigs over our mark-up!'

The second dealer is a bit stickier, but he still ends
up taking five pairs for three marks. 'Not bad either,'
Ludwig grins, outside. With the next dealer, it's
'Papa's just out getting a shave', and a fourth is only
willing to pay peanuts. 'Nothing doing, sir.' Ludwig
shows him the cold shoulder. 'Good wares for a good
price.' In the Grosse Hamburger Strasse, a woman
dealer buys up their remaining stock. Thirteen pairs.
Twelve pairs bought, the thirteenth thrown in, for
goodwill. She'll not buy thirteen, thirteen is unlucky.
But she pays a good price for twelve. Twelve marks.
The boys roll up their empty sacks, and their first
thought is to high-tail it out of the dangerous area.
On the bus they count their takings: twenty-two
marks and twenty-five pfennigs! Deduct their
investment of eight marks, leaves a profit margin of
fourteen marks and twenty-five pfennigs. 'All in one
day, Willi! And we've earned it!' Over a glass of beer
they relax and speculate on the future. And then

it's back to work. Today's harvest, twelve pairs, needs to be put in shape.

Frau Bauerbach asks what happened with registering with the police. Their exhilarated mood is quickly deflated. Did they really forget for the whole of one day that they are borstal youths, wanted by the police? They buy registration forms, fill them in with made-up details, and Frau Bauerbach has them countersigned by the concierge. She is grateful to the boys for offering to take them to the police station for her and saving her the journey. When they come back after a while and say, 'All done, Frau Bauerbach, we're legal,' they feel choked with anxiety. If she demands to see the officially stamped registration forms, they're toast. They'd have to go back to the gang. But Frau Bauerbach is a credulous soul. 'Lovely! Now, what about some coffee?' 'No, thank you, not just yet,' replies Ludwig, as his fear turns into quiet glee. That was close. Now, live discreetly and keep a lookout, and everything might still turn out okay.

The twelve pairs of shoes are fixed up and cleaned. For supper they treat themselves to some fresh rolls, butter and boiled ham. They've bought a few oranges as well. It's Christmas in a fortnight. Christmas? Where were we this time last year? Willi was in the institution. Ludwig needs to think about it for a long time. Then it comes to him: how could he have forgotten? Half-starved, and without an abode for a long time. If he managed to pick up two marks in the Tiergarten for sex, he felt rich. So rich that he could afford to eat for a day, and spend a night on a bedbug-infested mattress. 'Oh, Willi, if only we could stay here at Mother Bauerbach's . . . when I think about going back to the gang now . . . No, anything but that . . . anything but that!' They go to bed. The next day it's the turn of Kaiser-Friedrich-Strasse. 'Good morning. We're paying up to two marks . . .'

SIXTEEN

The Blood Brothers are increasingly turning into a gang of professional criminals. Hunger? A thing of the past! Running around in rags and with no home? We're past that. Fred, the influencer and seducer, has the gang firmly in his grip. Heinz and Georg, who to begin with put up some resistance, are dazzled by the amount of money so effortlessly earned, and all of them have now dismissed their doubts. Ludwig and Willi, the two prize idiots, have apparently got themselves nabbed again by the cops. The profitable pickpocketing excursions to department stores and weekly markets and market halls are continued.

But there are new opportunities too: break-ins, auto thefts! The loot always winds up back at godfather Gotthelf's, and is then farmed out to fences. Stolen cars are immediately driven by Fred (the only one who can drive) to some place in the provinces. There, there are various helpers' helpers, who spray the cars and move them on. A stolen car in good nick can bring in three to five hundred marks. And Fred won't even look at rotten cars. For instance, take the day before yesterday: the Adler that Fred picked up outside a bar in the West End. It still smelled of factory. Of course Fred filled her up and roared off down to Leipzig.

Jonny is sitting with the rest of the boys at godfather Gotthelf's on Badstrasse. They are waiting for Fred, he had reckoned to be back by six. Here comes a post cyclist with a wire for Gotthelf. 'Who's sending me love letters by express delivery then!?' Damn, that's Fred's writing, thinks Jonny. A scribbled note: *Jonny, the police are on my tail, but they're keeping their distance. Clear Badstrasse right away, and run. Go to Ulli's. If I can get away this time I'll see you there at midnight. Watch yourselves, maybe you have a visitor already. Fred.* They all stand there, trembling and pale. Only Gotthelf, the old jailbird, remarks casually: 'Oh, Gollnow's not such a bad place . . .' Jonny tells everyone to wrap the stolen loot, consisting mainly of ladies' silk stockings, into small parcels. Then he goes out on the street to see if there's any sign of the coppers yet.

He knows he can be arrested at any moment. Calmly he stands there in the doorway, puffs at a cigarette, and looks idly left and right. As usual in the early evening, there's a lot of people out and about on Badstrasse. But no sign of anything out of the ordinary. After a quarter of an hour, he gives orders for the goods to be shifted to Ulli's summer house. At intervals of a few minutes, the boys go off, one by one, each with a small parcel, to 80th Street, Section 2. As luck would have it, Ulli is home. In return for a share, he agrees to put up the goods and the Blood Brothers both. An hour later, the move is complete. Gotthelf's apartment is clean. Now let the cops come. 'A fence? What, me? You'd need to come up with some sort of evidence for that first, sirs.'

On the last trip to Ulli's, Jonny stops off and buys a roll of greaseproof paper. All the goods are wrapped up in that. A hole is dug behind the summer house: put all the stuff in there. Stamp it down, pour a couple of pails of gravel over the top. No sign of anything. So as not to betray the dark summer house, Ulli keeps the stove fed with coke, which produces a minimum amount of smoke. Four of the Brothers are sent out to buy two blankets apiece. There's no shortage of

169

money. To spend a winter's night in a summer house is a chilly pleasure. Rum and sugar are bought, and food. Before long, they're all sitting in front of a blazing stove, quietly discussing whether Fred will have managed to give the police the slip. The howling wind whistles, and rain lashes the small, thickly draped window. It's so warm in the summer house that the damp wooden walls are steaming.

It's long past midnight, and still no sign of Fred. The Blood Brothers are lying on their blankets, completely dressed. Who knows, they may have to scarper at a moment's notice. Finally, at almost two, there's the noise of a dog barking. It's Fred's signal! But the boys still don't make a move. Only when a solid object is scraped against the door, up and down, down and up, are they certain that it's Fred. Happy, totally wet through, but not in the least out of sorts, Fred flops on to a blanket. 'Hey there, boys! Just fix me up a grog first, will you?' He gulps down the hot strong drink and lights a cigarette. 'I laughed! I just went by Gotthelf's in a taxi. Have you any idea how many detectives are hanging around there? I saw three right off, two in the rain on the other side of the street in an entrance, and one in Gotthelf's passageway. Hunkered down in a corner, pretending to be an alkie! They must have been desperate to meet us . . .'

Once Jonny has put in that the goods are safe,

Fred starts to talk. The garage in Leipzig where he first took the car must have been under police observation, because from that point on he was always in company wherever he went. He of course couldn't go to the fellow who was supposed to take the car off his hands. By suddenly leaping on to a passing tram, he shook off the police. There they were again at the main Leipzig station, though they apparently missed Fred climbing on to the Berlin train. But then the Leipzig police must have wired Fred's details to Berlin, because when he got to Anhalter Bahnhof, there were two officers standing there who let him pass, but who then set off on his tail to find Fred's hidey-hole, and if possible his companions in crime as well. He wrote the wire on the hoof; luckily he had paper and stamps on him. And in the crush of Potsdamer Platz, an opportunity presented itself to post the letter unobserved. What set them on to the address in Badstrasse . . .

Anyway, it seemed the Blood Brothers had been under observation for some time now. Fred gave the officers the slip in the Friedrichstrasse branch of Aschinger's. The way to the toilets was down a corridor that led out to Krausenstrasse. The officers stood outside the Friedrichstrasse entrance, waiting for Fred to emerge. Waiting, waiting . . . Fred had avoided the area around Badstrasse and Koloniestrasse. Till he took that late-night taxi, and saw that their hiding place on Badstrasse was already surrounded.

'For the moment, you can stay here; it's not so bad, unless the weather turns really cold,' proposes Ulli. Ulli knows the Blood Brothers have money, and he'll do pretty much anything for money. 'Fred,' begins Jonny, 'you and I had better disappear for a few weeks till the hue and cry is gone. We could go to Magdeburg, and do the job there. You know the one . . . That's at least a couple of thou. The rest of you,' he turns to the other Blood Brothers, 'you can stay here, and carry on by yourselves. Only weekly markets, though. The department stores are getting twitchy. Ulli, how would you fancy a trip to Magdeburg? There's three hundred in it for you . . .' 'What's the job?' asks Ulli. 'A pretty harmless affair. I don't know the details. An old mucker of mine is in charge.'

Ulli says he's agreeable. Jonny gets everything ready for their departure on the early train. Konrad is to take over the gang during Jonny's absence. Ulli leaves his summer house to the Brothers staying in Berlin. The buried goods are to remain where they are. It's too risky to try and flog them now. A couple of brief hours of sleep. Fred, Jonny and Ulli pack a small travelling case each. Outside it's still pitch black and rainy. On Koloniestrasse they hail a taxi: 'Potsdamer Bahnhof.' Individually, with no sign that they know one another, they buy train tickets and board the train. Not until it moves off, and there are no signs of anything suspicious, do they link up. Thank God, they're clear of Berlin for the time being.

On reaching Magdeburg, Fred and Ulli wait in a breakfast place opposite the station, and Jonny goes off in search of his mate, one Frenchy Felix, who'd needed to get out of Berlin. Frenchy lives with his sweetheart on Fette-Hennen-Gasse. Where is Fette-Hennen-Gasse? On the Alter Markt, near the gaudy town hall. Fette-Hennen-Gasse is the Magdeburg equivalent of Berlin's Mulackstrasse. Only the warped little cottages in Magdeburg are a couple of hundred years older than those of the Berlin red-light district. Jonny picks his way up a steep narrow wooden stair; each step yields an inch or two, but complains with creaking and asthmatic wheezing. An unmistakable sign for the residents that there's a stranger about. The residents stick close to the wall when they go upstairs, and the stairs remain silent. At the top, it takes a very long time before there's an answer to Jonny's knocking. He can hear whispered consultation inside. 'Felix . . . it's Jonny here, Jonny from Berlin.' Thereupon the door is unlocked.

A bull of a man stands in front of Jonny, wearing a skimpy nightshirt: 'Jonny! Well, this is a surprise! Come in!' In the only bed, more alert and curious than demure, lies Felix's sweetheart, the prostitute Paula. Flattened corkscrew curls, in a fetching canary yellow, frame the delicate and attractive face. The great lunk Felix only likes to bestow his favours and protection on girls under fifty kilos. 'Are you here for the matter I think you're here for, Jonny?' 'Yes, Felix. I brought a couple of the boys with me. One you know: Fred.' 'Fred? He'll do.' Felix turns to his sweetheart: 'Cutey-pie, will you get up. My friend wants coffee, and so do I.' Cutey-pie jumps up, and first hurries to the mirror to sort out her hair. The rest, her delicate figure under the sheer nightie, she doesn't mind the boy seeing. Thank God everything's still where it ought to be, nothing roly-poly about her.

After breakfast Jonny and Felix head for Bahnhofstrasse, where Ulli and Fred are waiting. Felix and Fred know each other, but what about this other guy, Ulli? If Jonny's brought him, he's sure to be on the level. First thing, they leave the restaurant. Magdeburg is small. They talk over their plan in a quiet working-men's bar on Jacobstrasse. They'll need three days to case the house. The job is set for Saturday night. The place itself is no problem. The inhabitants have gone away, a cleaning woman comes once a week. There's nothing in the nature of an alarm. Sure, they won't be able to go through the front door, which is iron-plated inside and out, and the locks are new and sophisticated too. So there's no other way for it than in through the butcher's shop, and up through the ceiling. The butcher himself lives four doors away, and there's no one in the shop at night.

Kühleweinstrasse, just off Nordpark, lies there deathly quiet. A few isolated lights on in some of the houses. Magdeburg is a law-abiding town of sober habits, and Kühleweinstrasse doesn't buck the trend. At half past two in the morning, Felix and Jonny are standing outside the butcher's. The shop doesn't have any valuables, and isn't particularly well secured. The two locks on the door . . . well, put it this way, they're not the most challenging Frenchy's ever seen.

Ten minutes later, the door is open. A soft meow is the signal to Ulli and Fred, who've been standing guard on the corner. Ulli minds the door, the other three go to work inside. Everything happens quietly enough. Felix hops on to the counter, a little table supplies the extra height he needs to reach the ceiling. Fred and Jonny spread a blanket out. Felix's fretsaw attacks the ceiling. He's to saw out a square big enough for a person to pass through it. A tough job, even for the powerful Felix. At the end of half an hour, a plaster-of-Paris square falls noiselessly into the blanket the other two are holding ready. With a supple pull-up, Felix gets into the apartment. Jonny and Fred follow. Now everything's rosy, and time's not a problem. First get our bearings. Aha, the dining room. Cue: silver.

But everything's not as it should be. The fact that the butcher happened to have a little reunion tonight in Wilhelmstadt wasn't anything the band could have been expected to guess. He's just turning the corner into his street, when he sees a man posted in front of his shop. And the door – he has sharp eyes, even when he's coming home from a reunion – the door is ajar. A break-in at his shop! Police! Where to go? The bar on the corner of Rollenhagenstrasse still has its lights on. He rings up. 'Burglary!' The police pick up. '. . . but no sirens mind, officer, otherwise the villains will get away!'

But then the squad car does sound its siren! At some distance yet, but it's audible a long way off. Ulli hears it too, he yells into the shop: 'Out . . . out!' And now he needs to run. The butcher, in the shade of the opposite side of the street, is livid when he sees Ulli making a break for it. The police car screeches round the corner. Six officers, revolvers in hand, storm the shop, with the butcher lending moral support. Shining their powerful torches around, they quickly see the hole in the ceiling. Upstairs in the apartment, something tinkles to the floor. The leader of the police calls up: 'This is the police! Come down, or else we'll shoot!' Nothing moves. He calls up again. Then the officers hear the sound of a window being opened upstairs. The driver has switched on his mobile beam, and is now bathing the façade in harsh illumination. For a brief instant, a male figure can be made out by the window. The commander calls up again. From above comes an echoing reply: 'All right, we're coming down. Don't shoot.' One after the other, they clamber down into the shop through the hole. Shortly after, Jonny, Fred and Felix are sitting in handcuffs in the car. The apartment is searched, in case of any more villains lurking about. Since the door to the butcher's shop can no longer be secured, a constable is left on watch.

At last, the butcher can go to bed. His priceless sausages are safe, and the building's owner will pay for the hole in the ceiling. Not a bad advertisement for him, a break-in like that. On Monday, they'll come along in their swarms to stare at the hole in the ceiling. He could take advantage of that to put up a few prices here and there. Maybe his imperial huntsman's sausage could go up five pfennigs a quarter-pound. His account of the night's happenings is surely worth that much. He can imagine himself launching into it in front of his hushed clientele: '. . . so I see this fellow, a giant, a ruddy colossus, standing in front of my shop. Of course, I go right up to him. The fellow sees me coming, and draws a revolver. What choice do I

177

have? I have to knock him over before he gets a shot off at me . . .'

Ulli wanders around the unfamiliar city. His three mates have been nabbed, that's for sure. As he ran off, he could already see the flashing lights of the squad car. Luckily, Ulli had accepted an advance on the job from Jonny, otherwise he wouldn't even be able to make it back to Berlin. At five in the morning, he heads for the station, and takes a seat on the train to Berlin. By ten he's back in Koloniestrasse, and gives the signal outside his summer house. He knocks for a long time, finally they admit him. 'Hey Ulli! Where are the others? Jonny and Fred?' 'Where do you think they are? In police cells in Magdeburg . . .'

SEVENTEEN

The leading lights of the gang, Jonny and Fred, have been arrested. The rest of the boys, Konrad, Erwin, Heinz, Walter, Hans and Georg, are adrift, left to their own devices. Konrad, Jonny's stand-in, has nothing like the energy, the cold calculation, the intellect and the absolute ruthlessness of Fred or Jonny. And Ulli, head of the Seven of Spades, is a leader without a troop. His six pals have, by and by, drifted off to other gangs, or disappeared in the endless city. Anyway, Ulli isn't a leader of the type the gang members need. Like Konrad, he's impulsive, a born scrapper who loves a fight. But he doesn't have the

179

intellect that is Jonny's most striking quality. Each boy can sense it, however crudely, and shies away from such leadership.

Moreover, there's the fact that the rest of the gang feel the hot breath of the police down their necks. There are officers with orders to round up this band of youthful pickpockets and car-thieves. The knowledge of being on some wanted list or other was something they'd been familiar with over the years. You were a name among thousands of others. But this, this active pursuit, is intimidating and tends to irritate and cow them. They hardly dare set foot out of the summer house. Only under cover of darkness, on winter afternoons, do they slink out to buy food. The money they have won't last for more than another week. Fred was carrying the gang's fortune, well over five hundred marks, about his person. All of it is now in the hands of the Magdeburg police.

The morning of 24 December. They don't have a penny left. If they're not to go hungry on Christmas Eve and over the holidays, they have to go out and work. They will try their luck in the market hall on Ackerstrasse. Ulli wants no part of it. 'I'm doing enough for your welfare, letting you sleep here,' he says. He knows the Blood Brothers are utterly dependent on him and his summer house. Yesterday things had come to a head between Konrad and Ulli.

They move out in two groups of three and head for Ackerstrasse. The rendezvous afterwards is the Rückerklause. Ulli is staying home in the summer house.

The shoppers flocking around the stalls and in the narrow aisles afford plenty of easy pickings for the boys. But, in spite of that, they stand there and dither. They miss the dynamism of Fred and Jonny. Neither group can see the other. Then suddenly, in front of a fruit stand, a piercing cry: 'My money! My money!' The hysterical woman goes on and on. The screams provoke indescribable disturbance. Waves of excitement pulse through the space; no one thinks any more of buying or selling. 'Police! . . . My money . . . my money!' the bereft lady keeps wailing. Someone has called the police. The flying squad are coming . . . the flying squad are on their way, is the buzz throughout the crowd. Whoever has reason not to be there when they come makes for the Invalidenstrasse exit.

A minute later, six officers jump out of their vehicle. Two stand guard by the Ackerstrasse exit, two more on Invalidenstrasse. But what can six officers hope to do? Reinforcements are called. Half a platoon is bussed in. They go over the market hall with a fine-toothed comb. The market-sellers are livid, 'it's hurting my business'. Detained individuals swear and shout, a few bystanders with clean consciences find it all quite

181

diverting. A dozen suspicious characters are taken back to the station for questioning. The waves of agitation finally settle, and slowly the business rhythm reasserts itself. People go around warning each other: 'Take care . . . pickpockets! There's just been a huge police raid.'

Jonny's first and most essential principle was: as soon as there's the least excitement, just leave. Leave the department store, leave the market hall, leave the weekly market. One by one, at intervals of several hours, the Brothers congregate in the Rückerklause. It's already dark by the time all six are there. In the Rückerklause, the home for the homeless, the mood is mawkish and Christmassy. And when the loudspeaker intones: '*O du fröhliche, o du selige . . .*' the whole bar joins in. Not the sort of drunken growl that might accompany '*Liebe der Matrosen*', but in a decent, reverent, disciplined manner, as tuneful as can be managed. Sentiment, at the right moment, is not unwelcome to the hardest-hearted of ruffians. Tears, if shed in circumstances like these, have nothing weak or unmanly about them.

The cause of the kerfuffle in the market was Georg. 'Well, was it worth it at least?' Georg pulls out a purse: twenty-two marks. They split up and head back to the summer house on Koloniestrasse. At Gesundbrunnen station they stop off at a restaurant.

182

Walter is told to go get Ulli. They're still hacked off with him, but if they didn't have his summer house, they'd be really up against it. They sit over their fifty-pfennig suppers in silence. The restaurant's deserted, and there's not much going on outside, just people hurrying home. Walter returns, alone, out of breath, trembling. 'Ulli's gone . . . the summer house is locked up . . . there's a police seal on the door!' Five forks clank against plates. Police seal? Then they must have come for the gang, and found Ulli. It's over – over! Out of here. On to the underground and begone. Otherwise they'll be spending Christmas Eve behind Swedish curtains. The gang is finished. No place, hardly any money, the likelihood of arrest at any minute. They're sitting in an underground carriage in their ones and twos. They mustn't be seen to belong together. But they keep glancing up at each other, seeming to say: What do we do now?

Bachelors' Christmas Party, it says outside a little bar in a Bülowbogen side street. Half bar, half popular café. There's a tree with candles on it, and each table is decorated with fir twigs tied with coloured ribbons. The piano player keeps launching into 'Stille Nacht, heilige Nacht', as he should. A few street girls and their fancy men are getting drunk on punch and sentiment, and one half-lit individual is told off by the landlady for his tuneless bass. 'Sing it properly, you old disgrace . . .' The six Blood Brothers are seated next to the big Dutch oven, drinking their mulled wine and staring at the tree. Little Walter sheds a few big tears from his bulging eyes. He reaches up with his dirty hand to wipe them away, and now Walter has a properly grimy tear-stained orphan's face. When the first rush of Christmas feeling is over, the landlady remembers her tax arrears, and sets about bringing in more custom. Those six louts by the stove aren't eating anything, maybe they think this is a warming hall . . . 'What about some more mulled wine, boys?' 'Yes, ma'am.'

'I've got a place we can sleep, not much colder than the summer house. And there's blankets there too . . .' says Georg into the silence. 'Whereabouts?' 'Whereabouts?' they all chime in. 'Stallschreiberstrasse, doesn't cost a thing. I spent a whole week there one time . . .' It's almost midnight. The six Blood Brothers traipse off to their new billet, Georg's wheeze.

Stallschreiberstrasse, the stage entrance to the theatre on Kommandantenstrasse, closed for years. A low iron barrier separates the yard from the street. They're over it in a trice. Georg fiddles with a low door next to the stage entrance, and in no time he's picked the lock. They find themselves in a small theatre wardrobe. An open door leads out on to a narrow passage, which winds its way to the stage.

Georg lights the way with his torch. A few alarmed mice scuttle out of their path. A flight of stairs leads down to the heating cellar and various subterranean rooms where such things as sets and flats and pieces of furniture and so forth are stored. There's all kinds of things littered about. Also a few shot rugs, ends of carpet, backcloths and costumes mouldering away in various corners. The dream of one day standing up in the lights is one the rascals have long since kissed goodbye to. But as a place to kip, it's about as good as they can expect. In the everlasting night of this theatre basement the boys sleep long into Christmas Day. In uncertainty, in fear of what the future might bring.

They are condemned to spend the entire holiday holed up there. They can't very well go out into the yard and scramble over the fence in daylight. It's late in the evening when one of them is despatched to a bar somewhere to get something to eat. It's the same deal on Boxing Day. Two days and three nights in the dark and cold of the basement. By the time they venture out into the street, early the following day, none of them has a penny. Hungry, and rigid with cold, they wander into the warming hall on Ackerstrasse. They all have good winter coats – which they will now have to sell. Each of them gets three or four marks. Then back to the Rückerklause. Hot potato pancakes and a cup of broth. After dinner, each of them buys a half-pint. They need to make economies.

Only Heinz, who has barely spoken a word the past few days in the theatre, is ordering one schnapps after another. After paying, he's got thirty pfennigs left. 'Here, Erwin, this is for you. I won't be needing any money. Cos I'm . . . I'm on my way now . . . to the Alex . . . and hand myself in to the police . . .' Suddenly he starts wailing like a child, and his head drops on to the table. 'I've had all I can take . . . of this . . . this shitty life . . . I can't do it any more . . .' His friends try and comfort him, but he loses control completely. His body convulses with sobs. The other customers are making fun of him: 'Someone change his nappy, poor little baby's wet himself . . .' A pimp calls out to his sweetheart: 'Lotti, give the little boy your tit to keep him quiet . . .'

Finally, Heinz calms down. But he's set on going to the police. He puts on his cap. 'All the best, lads. You know I won't say anything about you . . .' 'Heinz, calm down!' 'Heinz, you're mad!' 'Stay, Heinz!' they appeal to him. Try to force him to stay. He breaks free, rushes out into the street. Konrad and Georg go after him. Heinz races to the unemployment office. There's always a policeman there. And his suspicion is borne out: there are two greens just turning the corner. Konrad and Georg have to stop if they are not to endanger themselves. Heinz is talking to the officers. Their first reaction is not to listen and to send him away, but they end up escorting him to the station.

Always quiet, always dreamy, Heinz had woken up. And his waking up, his insight into the way he and his friends have ended up, left him no option. He will be given the third degree. They will try to find out who he was with, what he's been doing. And if Heinz softens up, and confesses that he was part of the Blood Brothers, then the hunt will begin in earnest. But if Heinz remains stubborn, admits nothing and keeps the gang out of it, then he will be taken back to a home. The police will hardly be in a position to prove that he was involved in pickpocketing. If Heinz remains stubborn! However, if he allows his head to drop, and is softened up, and starts to sing . . . then the public prosecutor will be in business. The young offenders' court will shake their heads, and Heinz will be severely punished.

Heinz had woken up. And so horrible was his sense of a botched youth that prison or borstal appeared the lesser evil. He will certainly not attempt to run away from an institution again. Quietly, no longer dreaming, he will endure the torments of borstal life. On his twenty-first birthday – or perhaps sooner, with good behaviour – a spineless being, a cringing serf will leave the institution, and take up the cudgels against life. Heinz will fight with his hat in his hand.

Depressed and irresolute, the five remaining members of the gang wind through the streets. They no longer have the courage necessary for criminal deeds. Things will go back to being the way they were before Jonny, and before Fred. Prostitution for the odd thaler here or there, otherwise starve and starve. Homeless, homeless for such a long time that a mattress in a hostel seems like paradise. Or perhaps they will seek to join another gang. Working under a leader, picking pockets, small break-ins, car thefts . . . whatever this new gang specialises in.

Is there another way? Work, honest-to-goodness work? Even if such a miracle came to pass and someone came along asking 'Will you work for me?', it would be over as soon as it was asked! The papers! The official confirmation that so-and-so, born on such-and-such a date, is allowed to run around freely, and isn't condemned to be in a welfare home . . . this confirmation will break anyone's neck, because it hasn't been provided. Because they aren't allowed to run around freely. They are welfare kids, liable to be locked away, even if they've done nothing wrong! *To guard against falling into moral turpitude*, is what it says in the paragraph that delivers these minors into 'social provision'.

But the children, committed to the institution whose

function is to guard them against turpitude, only learn from their comrades how to make money in the easiest ways. How you make skeleton keys out of wire . . . how you crack a safe . . . how you break and enter a window without smashing glass . . . how and where you sell your body in Berlin . . . And: how you escape from the institution and make use of the things you've learned, or starve to death.

EIGHTEEN

Hundreds of thousands of unemployed are racking their brains for ways of making a living – for the basis of the most frugal existence. Thousands of new jobs come into being, jobs that could only have been thought up in sheer despair. From the man hawking pretzels round the bars, to the man who lends out umbrellas in unexpected rain showers. From 'watch your car, mister' to the 'Sherpa' in the garbage mountains on the edge of the city. A plethora of weird notions, sobering proof of a desire to remain honest, even in the teeth of the need to live and to eat.

This thing that eludes thousands: Willi and Ludwig

pulled it off right away. Their business, the buying and reconditioning of old footwear, has kept them fed. For two months now, they've been trekking around various parts of Berlin, parroting their sentence: 'We're paying up to two marks for . . .' On one occasion, they even did pay two marks. See, it happens. Someone had won a handsome pair of brown shoes in a trade-union tombola. For ten pfennigs. Unfortunately, though, the (un)lucky winner had size-eleven feet, while the shoes he won were a pair of tens. You do what you can for your union. You even wear shoes that don't fit, so as not to offend the secretary. Twice the winner wore the cheap but painfully tight shoes. Then, with a hideous curse, he flung them into a dark corner; from where, as related, they came to be in Ludwig's sack after two marks had changed hands. They were sold on for five . . .

Ludwig and Willi are sitting in their parlour at Frau Bauerbach's. They have just sold twenty-three pairs of shoes to dealers for a healthy margin. Their gang days are far, far in the past. There is a tacit agreement between them not to mention the Brothers. Nor have they run into any of them, either. From time to time they see a face that looks half-familiar. But they disregard it, and the fellow probably thinks he doesn't know them either. They no longer hang out in bars. Sure, they have the odd pint now and again, and they go to the cinema, but apart from that, they mind the pennies. So much so that, in the past two months, they've managed to put by one hundred and fifty marks. Frau Bauerbach gets her rent on the nail, and she is more than happy with her two 'brothers'. Also, the faked registration has yet to rear its ugly head. In Willi's case, the danger isn't that great anyway. In six months he'll be of age. Then he can get papers issued for himself. Ludwig, though, is only nineteen; they've got him for a good two years yet.

'Hey, Ludwig, we need to buy some more leather,' says Willi. 'Okay, let's do it right away.' They ride out to Invalidenstrasse. There's a leather business there where they pay wholesale prices. They buy ten pounds of scrap leather, plus some nails, and finally two proper cobbler's aprons. Their old sacking ones are in tatters. They walk over to catch the underground at Rosenthaler Platz. On the platform stands a young man. Willi and Ludwig don't notice him, but he recognises them both right away.

It's Hermann Plettner, the thief of the left-luggage ticket. He hasn't forgotten his ferocious beating in the summer house. Ludwig and Willi climb on to the train and sit down. Plettner follows them, but stays in the doorway, keeping an eye on them. He feels a burning rage. How can he avenge himself, principally on the fellow who shopped him to the gang? Ludwig.

The other fellow, Willi, was there as well when he was given his beating. When Ludwig and Willi get off at Neukölln, Plettner follows them. He sees them turn down Ziethenstrasse and disappear into Frau Bauerbach's basement, and not come back out. His plan is decided. He runs to the nearest telephone box, and asks to be put through to the Neukölln police. Even though he doesn't know anything about the two of them, he is sure that the police will be interested in Ludwig and Willi. Gang members are always in trouble with the law, he thinks. Not giving his own name, he tells the police the address on Ziethenstrasse . . . 'two people you want to see are living there. But you'd better hurry, because I don't know how long they're going to stay there.' He hangs up, and lights a cigarette. That's taken care of that then . . . the boys are finished.

Ludwig and Willi are just sorting through the leather scraps when there's a knock on the door. Frau Bauerbach is out having coffee with an acquaintance. Ludwig answers the door. Two gentlemen. 'Does Frau Bauerbach live here?' 'Yes.' 'Can we come in?' Once inside, the gentlemen identify themselves as detectives. Ludwig and Willi stand there like statues, even though they have a sinking feeling . . . sinking at a terrifying velocity into a bottomless abyss. 'You must be tenants here, is that right?' asks one of the detectives. '. . . yes . . . er, yes . . .' 'But we have no record of any tenants at Bauerbach's. Can we see your papers?' Papers . . . no record . . . Help! Who can help us?. . .

'We . . . er, I . . . don't have any . . . any papers.' 'What, no papers? What's your name then? And yours?' Willi gets a grip on himself and gives his details. The official consults his list of wanted persons. 'Aha. Absconded from the institution at H., and we're looking for you in connection with something else as well, is that right?' The other thing will be the beating that Friedrich took, thinks Willi. 'Yes.' 'What about you?' The detective turns to Ludwig. He gives them his details too. No point in trying the fake Kaiweit papers. 'What have you been doing with yourself all this time? What have you lived off?' the officer asks. Willi and Ludwig show off their cobbler's workshop, the pile of acquired shoes. They see a little spark of hope. Maybe they'll let us go, if they see we're working. The detective looks at his colleague. Both ask questions. How much did you earn from dealing shoes? Was it enough to live off?

Ludwig hurries across to the wardrobe. 'Here, Inspector, see this, one hundred and fifty marks, all of it money we've saved up. Come by honestly, from our work!' His hands pluck at the bills, he reckons up the silver money: 'We've led honest lives, and

194

worked hard, Inspector. And now you want to lock us up again?' He goes up to the detective, takes him by both arms: 'Leave us be . . . allow us to work! Give us some legal documents . . . please, Herr Inspector, please, please!' The officers can tell that Ludwig isn't trying to pull the wool over their eyes. 'Now sit down, boys, let's have a sensible chat.' Willi and Ludwig obediently sit, their eyes on the lips of the policemen. 'Do you want to know how we happened to find you?' 'No . . . no . . .' 'About an hour ago, you were denounced. A stranger called us, said a couple of wanted men were staying at this address. Do you have any idea who that might have been?' The boys look at each other: Do you know? Do you? 'No, Inspector.' They don't know. All they know is that it wasn't one of the Blood Brothers. But they're not going to mention them anyway; each of them is firmly set on that.

'Well, boys, I guess you know we're going to have to book you. Maybe the family court will let you go, once they hear you're in work. Pack a few things, we'll need to hold on to your cash for the time being, and then we'll go.' 'You can write your landlady a note saying you've suddenly had to go away,' suggests the other officer. Ludwig does so. *Dear Frau Bauerbach, we've had to go away for a week or two. Will you keep our things safe for us. Here's money for the next two weeks.* Mechanically they stuff the leather scraps back into the bag, move the latest acquisitions into a corner, and pack a few personal effects. 'All set?' 'I suppose . . .' 'Cheer up. It may never happen,' the officer attempts to comfort them.

It may never happen, Herr Inspector? What do you know about us? It's bad, it's awful. Now everything's finished again. You're sending us back to the institution. Before long we won't be able to stick it there any more . . . We'll run away again . . . we'll starve again, and finally wind up in another gang. You won't let us do proper honest work . . . You just want to harass us, and lock us away and beat us up . . . but help and support? No chance! 'Let's be having you, then.' They walk out, flanking one officer, the second following some way behind. They're no crooks, after all . . . whoever it was who denounced the boys is certainly a far greater villain, and definitely a miserable piece of work. In the station at Neukölln, a short statement is taken down. Tomorrow morning they'll be taken over to the Alex. Then they'll know more.

In response to their pleas, and intercession from the arresting officers, Ludwig and Willi are allowed to share a cell. Not two hours ago they were sitting in their parlour with cups of coffee, now a chilly cell is their abode. 'Who do you think shopped us, Willi?' asks a tormented Ludwig. They rack their brains, but they can't think of anyone mean enough to have done something like that. They spend the night without sleeping. The transition was too dramatic, too abrupt. They discuss a few practicalities, in the event that they are separated. Willi is to report the hundred and fifty marks as his exclusively – after all, he'll be out in six months.

Willi scoots up to Ludwig: 'You know, when I get out, then you can make a break for it again. We've got money. We'll meet up in Berlin, and stick together. We won't let them break us up.' 'But if I do run away, Willi, the first place they'll come looking for me is wherever you are. You'll have proper papers, you'll be registered. They'll find me right away,' Ludwig mutters, discouraged. 'Okay, so I won't register. We'll live somewhere, the way we lived in Ziethenstrasse. What's the worst thing that can happen? If they work out that I'm not registered, I'll get a fine, and we'll move somewhere else. If they catch you, then you just break out again. But we'll carry on with our business. Here, Ludwig, shake my hand, we won't let them grind us down. We won't go back to the gang, we've done all right with the shoes.' 'It would be nice if we were able to stick together, Willi. If I have a mate like you, then I won't worry about having to go back to Jonny's mob in the end.'

Early in the morning, the van takes them to

Alexanderplatz. Once again, Ludwig finds himself in the pen. It's Willi's first time in police detention. They are each taken to single cells. They've discussed everything anyway. The day after, Willi is brought before the investigating magistrate. 'There's a case against you for assault on the educator Friedrich. Then there's a demand from the institution at H. for your return. So you will be taken back there. A substantial sum of money – one hundred and fifty marks – was found on you. According to your statement, you came by it honestly. Tell me about it.' Willi tells him. He says nothing about past contacts with the gang. The magistrate takes notes, and Willi is taken away again.

Ludwig's statement tallies with Willi's. 'In all probability you will be found to have broken the terms of your parole, and will have to serve the balance of your sentence. Running away isn't usually thought of as compatible with probation.'

A few days go by. Ludwig and Willi are only able to see each other from a distance, during exercise in the prison yard. They are unable to communicate. One afternoon, Ludwig is again taken before the magistrate. 'We have made enquiries with your landlady on Ziethenstrasse. The woman has given you a glowing report. As a consequence, the juvenile court is prepared to find that you are not in breach of the terms of your probation. You will be taken back to H. tomorrow, with your associate Willi Kludas. But don't do any more stupid stunts, or attempt to run away. If you do, you'll have to serve the balance of your punishment.' Willi is told he is being taken back to the institution, and will then face charges of common assault.

The next morning, they see each other in the pen again. A police car takes them and their escorts to the railway station. As the train pulls out, Willi and Ludwig glance at each other: in six months' time we'll be back in Berlin.

NINETEEN

Late in the evening, the two escorts and their charges, Willi and Ludwig, arrive at the local train station. This is where, four months before, Willi crawled into the wood wool that was on its way to Cologne. At the station they are met by a vehicle from the institution, and they drive down the avenue along which Willi had run to freedom once: one, two, three, four . . . one, two, three, four . . . don't let up, Willi! Slowly, the wagon trundles back to the institution.

The inmates are already in their dormitories; Willi and Ludwig are taken in to see the director right away. The potentate first looks at the returned boys in silence.

He seems to have it in for Willi in particular, since it was Willi who had given Herr Friedrich his beating. He lights a cigar, and addresses Willi: 'You know, Kludas, that there's a case pending against you for assault?' 'Director, sir, you are not entitled to call me *"Du"*. I will only give you a reply if you address me appropriately. In six months' time I will be twenty-one,' Willi says with all the restraint he can muster, but the undertone of his speech is unmistakable. 'Well, there's a thing, the little lad here wants to be called *"Sie"*! My two layabouts!' Furiously the director shoots up out of his chair, and bangs his cigar down into the ashtray. 'What were you up to in Berlin? Don't tell me, you were thieving and whoring. And I'm to call you *"Sie"* for that? Would you mind telling me what you lived on, without papers? You, Ludwig, have been gone for almost two years, and you over four months.'

'Look in our files if you want to know. It's all in there, sir. We worked honestly. And Willi even put by a hundred and fifty marks!' Ludwig pouts. Willi won't say anything, but the corner of his mouth is twitching menacingly. The director will have seen what's going on with him. 'I'll read the report from Berlin, everything else will be decided in the morning.' He rings the bell. The teacher Friedrich appears. 'Herr Friedrich, your special friend Kludas here is to go in dorm one, and Ludwig in dorm two.'

Dormitory one is apparently fast asleep. No sooner has the sound of Friedrich's footfall echoed away, though, than things get going: 'Willi, Willi! They managed to nab you! Willi, when are you going to do a bunk next? Willi, I reckon Friedrich is due for another going over, will you help?' The questions hail down on Willi. White nightshirts cluster round his bed; four perch on the right side of his bed, four more on the left, two stand by the head, and another four at the foot. 'Willi, where did you go? Tell us all about it! What's Berlin like? Were there girls? Have you got a smoke? Go on, Willi, spill the beans! Where'd you get that silk scarf from? Look at that, Fritz, the fine gent's suiting, and the overcoat.' And Willi talks. He talks about his escape. How, instead of waking up in Berlin, he found himself just outside Cologne. He recalls Franz, his good friend the tramp, and describes the death ride under the express train.

The boys listen with bated breath. They are with him every step of the way. They are fighting at his side, fighting for their freedom. How Willi finally arrived in Berlin, the terrible first few days that followed. Then the meeting with Ludwig. He doesn't mention the Brothers. How he and Ludwig got lucky, and started making a bit of money. Till an unknown party denounced them to the police. He must have been a real bastard, they are all agreed on that. 'Well, six more months. Then I'm out of here,' Willi ends his account. Of course he doesn't say anything about his compact with Ludwig either. There are spies everywhere, like Blaustein. He asks after Blaustein. 'Blaustein? They let him go. He was the governor's pet canary, after all.' That night, not much sleeping gets done in dormitory one. The boys lie awake in their beds, and relive Willi's adventures for themselves.

'That's why I'd like to ask you to leave Kludas relatively unscathed, gentlemen. I'd really prefer not to have to go through crisis after crisis during the few months the lout is still with us. He's completely out of control, I could tell that right away yesterday. Why go to such lengths over such anti-social elements? He'll be up before the court soon enough in connection with the Friedrich case. Let's hope he gets put away for a few months, and then we'll hardly have him here at all. At any rate, I intend to give him such a character witness as to exclude any possibility of probation. That's it, gentlemen.' The director calls the meeting to a close.

At first, Willi and Ludwig don't get much chance to talk undisturbed. A teacher always breaks them up immediately: 'What are you two conspiring about?' Four weeks pass of the usual constant trot. Any stirrings of individuality are brutally crushed. There are no exceptions, everyone has to do as the institution says. Why treat them as individuals? When they leave, all they'll do is go on the state anyway.

One day, Willi is sent the charge sheet from the juvenile court. Actual bodily harm. Ten days later, two masters accompany him to court. He is the only accused, none of the other identities could be established. Herr Friedrich gives evidence, and refers to 'chronic impairments of health that are still with me today'. The headmaster gives the court his sense of Willi's character. Willi is rough, stubborn, and violence is his element. He represents a constant danger to the institution.

'Accused, do you at least feel any remorse for your ugly action?' asks the judge. 'Do you want me to tell the truth, Your Honour?' 'Why, naturally!' 'Your Honour, I don't. Herr Friedrich tormented us too much,' says Willy, cutting himself off from any possibility of a lighter sentence. His outspokenness is very much to the headmaster's liking. Now he can be sure of getting shot of the boy. '. . . I therefore call for a sentence of three months in prison. Further, I would like to ask expressly that the accused – whose coarseness bears out the headmaster's account of his character – be denied probation,' argues the prosecutor, incensed.

'The accused is sentenced to two months. The court was not able to find any mitigating circumstances, seeing as the accused expressly stands by his actions.'

Willi's punishment begins three weeks later.

By the time Willi has served his term in prison and is returned to the care of the institution, he's just three weeks and two days from his twenty-first birthday. Three weeks and two days till freedom! It's getting to be time to make a detailed plan with Ludwig. During a free period one afternoon, they're strolling across the yard together. 'Ludwig, I'm going to go straight back to Ma Bauerbach's in Berlin, and sell those shoes we've got left. They'll bring in at least twenty-five marks. We've still got a hundred and fifty, comes to one hundred and seventy-five. The following day I'll come back here, I'll rent a bicycle and I'll wait for you at 8 p.m. You go over the wall, and we rush into town on the bicycle, give it back, and take the next train to wherever it's going. Just to get out of the area. And then we go to Berlin. When they let me go here, I'll get one free ticket to Berlin. The return here, and tickets for us both to Berlin will cost about sixty marks. That will leave us with about a hundred. But that's okay, we'll earn it back, in Berlin. How's that sound to you, Ludwig?' Ludwig looks at his friend who, on his account, is prepared to live unregistered with him, wanted by the authorities. 'Okay, Willi.' They shake on it.

The day before Willi's departure, they iron out the last few details: where Willi will be waiting with the bicycle, what time Ludwig is going over the wall. The headmaster asks to see Willi when he is released. 'Here's your money, one hundred and fifty marks. Here's a ticket to Berlin. And now, Herr Kludas, all that remains is for me to hope that you may still one day become a useful member of society. Goodbye.' 'Bye.'

A June day, lovely and succulent, greets Willi. And Willi greets it back; but his greeting to freedom, his drowning in the incomparably lovely summer's day, is brief and rushed. Quick, off to the city, mustn't miss the train. Pleased? Sure, Willi's pleased. But there's still someone else stuck inside, namely Ludwig, and he wants to get out and feel free as well. First he wants springing. Once they're both safely back in Berlin, then there's all the time in the world to relish their situation. Hurry, hurry. Don't fret, Ludwig. I'll be there for you.

There's the express standing there. No, no need to crawl under the wood wool this time. On the train is cushier than underneath. Let's go, driver! What are we waiting for? Ludwig wants to eat pea soup at Aschinger's!

Berlin: Anhalter Bahnhof. A huge human wave spills out of the boiling-hot compartments, floods the platform, greets and is greeted, calls for porters, blubs happily into handkerchiefs, and surges noisily into the station hall. There is still a little daylight, and Askanischer Platz is flashing in the light of electric suns, and the bubbling of advertisements. A summer evening, warm but not too warm. People are in less of a hurry than usual. The air is pleasantly tiring, women and girls rest softly and warmly in the embraces of men.

What do I care about all this, thinks Willi. Got to get myself to Mother Bauerbach's, Ziethenstrasse, Neukölln. Maybe she'll let me sleep there, if she's not re-let the room. Tomorrow morning, bright and early, flog shoes, then run back to the train. Ludwig will be waiting tomorrow at eight.

In Ziethenstrasse the 'To Let' sign is hanging out. 'Evening, Frau Bauerbach.' 'Oh, it's you, Herr . . . Herr . . .' 'My actual name is Kludas, Frau Bauerbach.' 'I thought you were . . .' 'Freed, Frau Bauerbach, freed. Here's the stamp to prove it. And I'm now adult.' Among Berlin landladies, Frau Bauerbach is such a rare specimen she probably deserves to go in a museum. Anyone else would have slammed the door in the convict's face. Frau Bauerbach asks and asks away and she cries a nice little tear when she learns that Ludwig is still looking at a whole year in the institution. 'Would it be all right if I stayed the night here? I'll take out the shoes tomorrow, and then I'll be on my way.' 'But of course, Herr Kaiweit . . . Herr . . . Kludas, of course.'

At eight o'clock the next morning, Willi is with the dealers, hawking his shoes. Why is it so long since he was last round, he is asked. 'Been sick, master, been sick. First I had measles, then I went away as a journeyman,' Willi lies smoothly. 'But now we'll be back, regular-like. What will you give me for the whole lot?' 'For everything? I'm not sure I want it. Let's have a look.' 'What about thirty marks,' suggests Willi. In the end he gets twenty-eight, which he is very happy with.

What's the time now? Just a bite to eat, then back to Mother Bauerbach's, to pick up his baggage and say goodbye. Then leave the suitcase at the station, and get on the express. Ludwig will be trembling with impatience. You reckon I might not make it? That's all you know, chum! Hope I can get a bike in that dump.

He does. 'What's the deposit on a bicycle?' 'Fifty marks.' 'Got it here. Can I have a receipt . . . ? Now, I aim to be back in three hours.' He gets on the old boneshaker and sets off in Ludwig's direction. It's getting to be time. Ludwig will be sniffing to see if the coast is clear. Get on over the wall, Ludwig! I'm on my way! Come on, come on! The bike's going nicely . . . Cut through the village, and then the borstal heaves into sight. Come on . . . come on! There at the back, under the clump of trees, that's my spot.

Stand the bike against the tree, ready to go. Look out for Ludwig . . .

Here he comes! He's running! Look at him go! He's racing . . . and racing! 'Ludwig!' 'Willi! . . . Willi!' The tears are streaming down his cheeks. 'Get on the luggage rack, Ludwig! You ready?' 'Yup.' 'Okay! Go, go, go!' 'Willi . . .' 'Save it for later, I need to pedal!' And push . . . and push . . .

'There's your bike back, chief. Went like a dream . . .' The station. When's the next train? It's eight-oh- . . . In six minutes. Wrong direction. Who cares? Get out of here. They've got the compartment to themselves. 'All aboard!' 'Here you go, Ludwig, ciggy to chomp on.' Rat-ta-ta-TA, rat-ta-ta-TA . . . They have to spend the night in the place the train ends up. They eat dinner in a simple restaurant, raise a glass to health and happiness, and then go to sleep. Early next morning, there's a train to Berlin.

And then it's Anhalter Bahnhof again. Once again, they spend the night in a small hotel, and propose to look for a room the next day in the area of Görlitzer Bahnhof. They will claim to be the Kludas brothers; no hope of any police registration, of course. Too bad, really, Ma Bauerbach was such a nice landlady . . . On Wiener Strasse they find something suitable. A half-deaf tailor, another basement flat. The room is so big that they can use a corner of it as a workshop.

'How much is the room for the two of us?' they yell into the tailor's ear. The old fellow doesn't want much. Eight marks a week. And Herr Kratochvil has no objection to their profession as boot-buyers. They go back to Anhalter Bahnhof and pick up Willi's suitcase and their gear. Of course, Ludwig has had to leave his clobber in the institution. 'We'll buy new stuff,' Willi comforts him. They spend the day straightening up the room and setting up the workshop. In the evening they sit up for a long time in their new home, wondering which streets they will go to tomorrow, to relieve them of their old footwear.

TWENTY

Comprehensively powdered with the fine dust of country roads, hungry and thirsty and falling-over tired, a young lad slinks along Linienstrasse at midnight, turns down Rücker, and slopes into the Klause.

It's Fred, who seven months ago was picked up in Magdeburg, along with Jonny and Frenchy Felix. The juvenile court in Magdeburg sentenced Fred – who had no prior convictions – to eight months in prison. Then he was taken to the Berlin authorities. For a car theft. He was suspected of being involved in many other crimes. But, in Berlin, Fred had a great stroke of luck. The people in Leipzig who had watched Fred weren't able to maintain with hundred per cent certainty that this was the man who delivered that car to the garage. Since Fred denied everything, had seen Jonny but didn't know him, and had never been a member of any gang, the court had to acquit him for lack of evidence. Thereupon the court in Magdeburg gave him half his sentence off on probation. Fred did four months and was then shipped on to a juvenile detention centre outside Berlin.

From his first day there, Fred thought of nothing but getting out. It took him two months before he could. And now, back in Berlin, he is looking for his gang, for the Brothers. There's no one in the Rückerklause. The place is almost empty. The regulars are dotted about the woods and lakeshores around Berlin. Only when their tummies rumble do they visit the city and spend a day or two scrounging food. No Blood Brothers at Schmidt's on Linienstrasse either. Finally, in Max's next door, there's Konrad on his tod with an orangeade. 'Hey, Konrad . . .' 'Fred . . .! Fred! Where've you sprung from?' Fred picks up Konrad's glass and empties it. 'Where from? What do you think, I made a break for it!' 'From jug?' 'No, welfare. Have you got funds, Konrad? I'm starving . . .'

Konrad has a two-mark piece, and half of that is for Fred. They walk round to Aschinger's on Rosenthaler

Platz. Fred wolfs down a bowl of pea soup and cleans out the bread basket. A small beer, a couple of cigarettes, and the money's all gone. But Fred is himself again. Fred, who had steered the fortunes of the gang, back in the day when everyone had a fistful of bills in his pocket. 'Where're the others then?' he asks. Konrad can only shrug. Heinz surrendered to the police. Walter and Hans were picked up three months ago. Georg is pimping for a bird. Has a snazzy wardrobe and boozes away the cash she brings home in the bars around Bülowbogen. And Erwin, he's on the game hereabouts, on Rosenthaler Platz. One mark a pop . . . down in the gents. They collared Ulli, too, in his summer house on Christmas Eve. And as for himself, Konrad, he's not exactly on top of his game. A mark here, a thaler there. No news of Ludwig or that other guy, Willi.

Fred has a think. 'That means there's just you and Erwin and me . . . okay, let's get a couple of recruits. Jonny's going to be a while. They gave him eighteen months down in Magdeburg.' Konrad is full of enthusiasm for Fred. Erwin, too, whom they run down in the Schnurrbart-Diele on Gormannstrasse, is ready to throw in his lot with Fred right away. It's a warm night; they spend it in Friedrichshain park.

The next day, Fred and Konrad and Erwin get to work. Fred seems to have forgotten nothing in the seven months he was gone. A couple of hours later and he has three purses. Forty-two marks. And by that evening there's six gang members. They're sitting at Raband's on Elsässer Strasse. Fred has been appointed gang leader. The Blood Brothers are back in business. And along with them, hundreds of other gangs and bands up and down the length of the Berlin road.*

And Willi and Ludwig? They're back with their tailor near Görlitzer Bahnhof. Buying and selling old boots and shoes, and making a reasonable living. Their gangland time is in the past, forgotten. But they still suffer from having to live unregistered. Any minute could be their last together. For another year Ludwig has to have the sword of Damocles over his head, from having absconded from his borstal. Calamity could strike at any moment, the police might come for him and take him away.

These two, who have gone through every sort of hell and limbo to escape from welfare. The sort of upbringing that claims to guard against moral turpitude. The soprano with milk teeth next to the gangland *routinier*. The fifteen-year-old virgin – she shoplifted the odd ribbon, some glass beads or chocolates in a department

---

* 'Landstrasse Berlin': this, Haffner's original title, conflates Berlin and the 'high road' of tramps and allegory.

store – next to the young prostitute who already has her first dose and Salvarsan cure behind her . . .

The poisons that are bred from the indiscriminate mingling soon make themselves evident. The boy has learned from his pals that as a fair-haired pale-skinned underage youth, he doesn't have to learn the ins and outs of stealing or breaking and entering if he runs away. On Friedrichstrassenpassage or in Tiergarten a boy like that can earn – quite literally – a pretty penny. Even in the institution a boy like that may receive the odd amenity. At night, in the dorm. The big twenty-year-old lunks lie in their beds, unable to sleep with their imaginations heated by fantasies of the other sex.

Willi and Ludwig stick together like burrs – they need each other. Without Willi, Ludwig would be on the brink. And Willi knows that he needs his chum.

Berlin – endless, merciless Berlin – is too much for anyone on their own. They felt over numberless nights what it means: to trudge alone through sleeping streets. Trudging . . . trudging. Mechanically setting one foot before the other . . . one . . . foot . . . be . . . fore . . . the . . . other . . . Till the exhausted machinery fails and you find yourself slumped in a doorway somewhere. Not for long. Because a police patrol comes past. Taps you on the shoulder: 'Oi, you! Haven't you got a home to go to? You can't sleep here.' 'Er . . .

what? Home? Course . . . course . . . I just dropped off. I'm on my way, officer, I'm on my way . . .'

If there's two of you, it feels different. A night is only half as long and half as cold; even hunger is only half as bad. One gives the other a nudge in the ribs: 'Well, what about it? Let's go! Two trips from Schlesischer Bahnhof to Charlottenburg, and the night's over.'

Willi and Ludwig can afford to laugh. But the glum sense that, even now, some Hermann Plettner or other could steer the police their way, that never quite lets them go. The time till Ludwig's twenty-first birthday will cost them a few anxious moments yet. Willi and Ludwig, two out of the wretched army of big-city layabouts, who even as they were about to be washed away, weren't washed away. Two of thousands on the Berlin high road.